Ithaca Forever

Itaca per sempre

Ithaca Forever

Penelope Speaks, A Novel

Luigi Malerba

Translated by Douglas Grant Heise

UNIVERSITY OF CALIFORNIA PRESS

University of California Press, one of the most distinguished university presses in the United States, enriches lives around the world by advancing scholarship in the humanities, social sciences, and natural sciences. Its activities are supported by the UC Press Foundation and by philanthropic contributions from individuals and institutions. For more information, visit www.ucpress.edu.

University of California Press
Oakland, California

Library of Congress Cataloging-in-Publication Data

Names: Malerba, Luigi, author. | Heise, Douglas Grant, translator.
Title: Ithaca forever : Penelope speaks, a novel / Luigi Malerba translated by Douglas Grant Heise.
Description: Oakland, California: University of California Press, [2019] |
Identifiers: LCCN 2018059055 (print) | LCCN 2019003057 (ebook) | ISBN 9780520972810 | ISBN 9780520303683 (cloth : alk. paper)
Subjects: LCSH: Homer. Odyssey. English—Fiction. | Odysseus, King of Ithaca (Mythological character)—Fiction. | Penelope (Greek mythological character)—Fiction.
Classification: LCC PQ4873.A42 (ebook) | LCC PQ4873.A42 I8513 2019 (print) | DDC 853/.914—dc23
LC record available at http://lccn.loc.gov/2018059055

Manufactured in the United States of America

26 25 24 23 22 21 20 19
10 9 8 7 6 5 4 3 2 1

The publisher and the University of California Press Foundation gratefully acknowledge the generous support of the Constance and William Withey Endowment Fund in History and Music.

Douglas Grant Heise would like to express his thanks to PEN America for its support of this translation through the 2017 PEN Grant for the English Translation of Italian Literature.

PREFACE

Luigi Malerba—born Luigi Bonardi but better known by his pseudonym—was born in November 1927 in Berceto, an Italian village in the Parma Apennines. Although he studied law at the University of Parma, he quickly became interested in cinema and soon began a collaboration with the Italian critical journal *Cinema,* bringing out his own series titled *Sequenze,* or "Sequences: Notebooks on Cinema." He moved to Rome in 1950 and began working in screenwriting and directing, before publishing, in 1963, the novel *La scoperta dell' alfabeto* (The Discovery of the Alphabet). This was followed in 1966 by *Il serpente* (The Snake) and in 1968 by *Salto mortale* (Somersault), which was nominated by Italo Calvino for—and won—the first Prix Médicis in 1970. A distinguished and highly varied literary career followed, including the award of an honorary degree in Italian literature from the University of Parma in 1990 and the publication of *Itaca per sempre* (Ithaca Forever) with Mondadori in 1997. When Malerba died in May 2008, he left behind a corpus of more than forty literary works, which have been translated and published all over the world, and a reputation as one of the central figures of Italian twentieth-century writing.

Although Malerba has been given many labels, he is a notoriously difficult writer to categorize. He was associated for a time with the Italian literary movement Gruppo 63, a group of neo-avant-garde intellectuals and writers who first came together during a 1963 meeting in Palermo. And yet, as Michael Caesar writes," [Malerba] has never allowed himself to be captured by any single tendency or set of problems... [as an] author [he] is far too canny to allow himself to be stuck on any one track."[1] Umberto Eco—himself a founding member of the Gruppo 63—sketches out the author's many connections to postmodernism in his retrospective on Malerba, even as he refuses to pin him down as a postmodern writer per se.[2]

Certain features of Malerba's work and style, however, stand out. The first and perhaps most conspicuous is Malerba's focus on the slippage between fiction and reality, and his ability to play in his fiction with the boundaries between the two until they become indissoluble. His writing is filled with ironies and ambiguities, evidencing themes of disconnection and uncertainty in his earliest works; as Malerba commented, "In the end, fictions and reality are mixed together."[3] In attempting to characterize Malerba's "brilliant art of lying" as (at least in part) postmodernist, Eco gives

1. Michael Caesar, "Contemporary Italy (since 1956)," in *The Cambridge History of Italian Literature*, edited by Peter Brand and Lino Pertile (Cambridge: Cambridge University Press, 1997), 559–606.

2. Umberto Eco, "Luigi Malerba visto da Eco: La genial arte della menzogna," *La Repubblica Parma*, October 8, 2009, https://parma.repubblica.it/dettaglio/luigi-malerba-visto-da-eco-la-geniale-arte-della-menzogna/1742818/3.

3. Paolo Mauri, "L'Odissea Di Luigi Malerba," *La Repubblica*, March 20, 1997, https://ricerca.repubblica.it/repubblica/archivio/repubblica/1997/03/20/odissea-di-luigi-malerba.html.

a definition of postmodernism that captures Malerba's artful exploration of the gaps and limits of fiction: "Postmodernism accepts modernism's refutation of the traditional notion of well-constructed narrative, but does not reject its formal features, except that it makes a counterattack, falsifying them, nullifying them, while the reader believes that they have been put to work to delight them."[4] Giovanni Accardo, meanwhile, describes Malerba's style as "a game that constantly mixes truth and lies, confounding fiction and reality, literary tradition and its reinterpretation" (p. 307).[5] This observation highlights another feature of Malerba's writing: its learned intertextuality. *Ithaca Forever* is, of course, a reworking of Homer's *Odyssey* that engages deeply not only with the source text but also with scholarship on the *Odyssey*. Indeed, Malerba notes in his postscript that the idea for the novel arose from a discussion at Cornell University with Pietro Pucci, a noted Homerist. But *Ithaca Forever* is not Malerba's only novel to engage in literary citation and intertextual games. In *Salto mortale* (1968), for example, we have a parody of Vergil's *Aeneid,* and in *Il protagonista* (1973) a response to Dante's *Vita Nuova*[6]—both of whom (Vergil and Dante) were themselves receivers of Homer.

It is thus to the intertextuality of Malerba's *Ithaca Forever* in particular—its relationship both to Homer and to other reworkings of the *Odyssey* —that we turn next.

Luigi Malerba was a polymath, interested in many different subjects, media, and approaches, from cinematography to journalism, from the power of language to the problems of politics.

---

4. Eco, "Luigi Malerba visto da Eco."

5. Giovanni Accardo, "Il senso della realtà nell' opera di Luigi Malerba," *Studi Novecenteschi* 39, no. 84 (2012): 279–314.

6. Francesco Muzzioli, "Luigi Malerba," *Belfagor* 44, no. 5 (1989): 521–37.

Above all, he was fascinated by the interconnection between lies and fiction: the power of stories to deceive and belie our expectations. Perhaps it was natural, then, that toward the end of his literary career he should be drawn to Odysseus, the "man of many wiles," notorious for his cunning and capacious inventiveness.

Malerba's *Ithaca Forever* begins at the point, in book 13, where Odysseus arrives on Ithaca, alone, disorientated, unable to recognize his homeland. Whereas Homer has the island disguised from Odysseus by Athena's mist, and soon revealed to the hero, this Ithaca is a strange one that Odysseus "know[s] should be Ithaca, but which [he] do[es] not recognize" (p. 1). It is a land of strange, "red sponge-like rocks" (p. 1), "arid and wild" (p. 2) and circled by hawks, quite different from the verdant island he remembers. The novel opens, then, in uncertainty and indeterminacy, the gods absent, Ithaca unrecognized. The opening departure from Homer's Odysseus, vouchsafed the knowledge of his homeland and sure of his return, sets a tone of troubling uncertainty and disruption that both mirrors the discord on land and begins a pattern of misrecognition and doubt that continues throughout the novel.

Ithaca's identity is, however, confirmed a few pages later, not by a god as in Homer—Athena is conspicuous by her absence, and the gods in this story "are distant" (p. 12)—but by the swineherd Eumaios, who tells him, "This is Ithaca, the homeland of Odysseus" (p. 8). And as Odysseus gains certainty about his location on Ithaca, we move back to more familiar territory, following the plot line of the *Odyssey* with meticulous faithfulness. Odysseus meets with his son Telemachus; he takes on his disguise as a beggar (here, a decision made by Odysseus and not the gods, as a means to test Penelope); he returns to the palace, wins the contest of the bow, slays the suitors, and engages in the prolonged recognition with Penelope, culminating in his reinstatement to his position within Ithaca.

On the surface, then, Malerba's version is very similar to Homer's narrative—and on the face of it the author is assiduous in his fidelity to the *Odyssey*, at times matching Homer scene for scene and almost word for word. Yet it is the very similarity of Malerba's *Ithaca* to Homer that lures us into a false sense of security, for as the novel progresses, the slight alterations that first appeared to hint at its difference from Homer—the absence of the gods, the unrecognizability of Ithaca—start to diverge into rifts that pry open gaps in the Homeric narrative.

One of the best-known controversies surrounding Homer's *Odyssey* is that of the characterization of Penelope, and in particular the question of when Penelope recognizes the disguised beggar as Odysseus. Penelope's character is notoriously ambiguous in the ancient epic, often apparently passive as she waits for Odysseus to return home—her son Telemachus describes her as "neither denying a marriage that would be hateful to her, nor able to put an end to all this" (*Od.* 1.249–50, 16.126–27). At times she seems to have recognized the disguised beggar as Odysseus, as when, for example, she comments on the beggar's similarity to her long-lost husband (19.358–60); at others, she seems to encourage the suitors in their contest for her hand, beautifying herself "to make their hearts flutter" (18.160–61). The recognition between Penelope and Odysseus is delayed again and again, in spite of several conversations between them in which they exchange news of Odysseus and portents of his return, and despite Odysseus' recognition by his nurse, Eurycleia, as she washes him and notices a familiar scar (19.386–498). Then Penelope, immediately after Odysseus the beggar has predicted his own return, announces a contest for her hand: the suitor to string Odysseus' bow and shoot an arrow through the handles of twelve axes will become her husband. Does this mean that Penelope has recognized Odysseus and is giving him the opportunity to win her back? Or has she given up at the very moment at which she has been told Odysseus will return? Homer is silent.

At last, having succeeded in the contest of the bow and killed the suitors (books 21–22), Odysseus makes his return known (book 23), and Penelope—doubting his identity yet again—finally confirms it with the test of their marriage bed (23.173–206). A reunion follows between the husband and wife in which they tell each other what has happened in their absence (23.241–87); the next day, Odysseus leaves to visit his aged father, Laertes, who also, like Penelope, recognizes Odysseus through certain signs (the scar on his leg and the identification of the number of fruit trees in the orchard [24.330–44]). The families of the suitors who were killed by Odysseus gather against him, but Athena intervenes and puts an end to the violence, restoring Odysseus to his rightful place as king of Ithaca.

The *Odyssey* of Homer, then, prolongs the recognition between Odysseus and Penelope over six books (that is, a quarter of the poem)—leading scholars to ask exactly why it takes Penelope so long to recognize her husband. Is it an artifice of plot, designed to maximize the climactic moment of Odysseus' revelation? An ambiguity or indeterminacy in Penelope's characterization, designed to keep her options—and her interpretation—open?[7] Or does she in fact recognize Odysseus as the beggar as early as

---

7. Nancy Felson, *Regarding Penelope: From Character to Poetics* (Norman: University of Oklahoma Press, 1994).

book 19—and dissimulate in order to join with Odysseus in gaining vengeance on the suitors?[8]

It is these questions—or "narrative discrepancies," as Malerba puts it (p. 135)—that drive *Ithaca Forever*. Malerba himself, in an interview for *La Repubblica* shortly after the publication of *Ithaca*, commented: "I did not want to correct the *Odyssey*, but to tell what Homer—purposefully, and deceitfully—does not say about Odysseus and Penelope.... And then there is Penelope's passivity, which isn't credible and begins the ancient Greek misogynistic tradition" (Mauri 1997). The crux of the departure from Homer is in the staging of the novel as two competing monologues between Odysseus and Penelope. We are therefore (in line with other modern reworkings of the *Odyssey* that have focused on Penelope's voice[9]) allowed an insight into Penelope's thoughts and voice that sets her apart from the veiled Homeric Penelope—and that enables us, in turn, to pinpoint the exact moment at which Penelope recognizes Odysseus ("When I heard this vagabond's voice for the first time, and locked eyes with him for a single instant, I knew" [p. 40]).

At first it might seem that this certainty of the moment of recognition reduces the ambiguity and polyvalency of Homer's *Odyssey*, but in fact it is quite the opposite. Now able to hear both

8. See, for example, Philip Whaley Harsh, "Penelope and Odysseus in *Odyssey* XIX," *American Journal of Philology* 71, no. 1 (1950): 1–21; see also John B. Vlahos, "Homer's *Odyssey*, Books 19 and 23: Early Recognition, a Solution to the Enigmas of Ivory and Horns, and the Test of the Bed," *College Literature* 34, no. 2 (2007): 107–31.

9. Sheila Murnaghan, "Reading Penelope," in *Epic and Epoch: Essays on the Interpretation and History of a Genre*, edited by Steven M. Oberhelman, Van Kelly, and Richard Golsan (Lubbock: Texas Tech University Press, 1994), 76–96. See also Emily Hauser, "'There Is Another Story': Writing after the *Odyssey* in Margaret Atwood's *The Penelopiad*," *Classical Receptions Journal* 10, no. 2 (2018): 109–26.

Penelope's and Odysseus' voice, we are caught in a "game of fictions" (p. 41) as Odysseus assumes that Penelope has not recognized him—and Penelope decides to pretend it is so in order to avenge Odysseus' mistrust of her. The reliability of the narrative voice is gradually called into question as "the two main characters recount events, each from their own point of view, in a proliferation of the narrating voice which ends by destroying any hierarchy of facts given in the narrative, and casts doubt on the idea of truth itself."[10]

A dissonance starts to open up between the two narrators as Odysseus acts a fiction dictated for him by Penelope, and Penelope lies to force Odysseus to reveal himself of his own accord. Through Penelope, we gain a psychological angle on Odysseus' Homeric dissimulation and propensity for tricks and cunning: traumatized by his experience of the war and his travels, "he is now suspicious of everyone everywhere ... he goes looking for obstacles everywhere, and when he does not find them, he invents them himself, as if he wanted to test his own craft and intelligence time and time again" (p. 47). Indeed, in a moment of intertextual self-reflexivity, it is precisely Odysseus' propensity for tale telling and lies that Malerba's Penelope identifies as the trait by which she recognized him (p. 100).

Penelope's continued refusal to recognize the beggar, meanwhile, leads first Telemachus and then herself and even Odysseus into a dizzying spiral of doubt and uncertainty: "Her words disoriented me," Odysseus comments (p. 110), finding his identity just as slippery as the uncertainty with which he approached Ithaca. His defeat by Penelope's dissimulation is then read by Penelope as uncharacteristic of the real Odysseus, confirming her fiction

---

10. Accardo, "Il senso della realtà," 306–7.

that he is not, in fact, Odysseus: "My falsehood thus runs the risk of coinciding with an alternative possible truth, and my mind is confused" (p. 123). Truth and lies, the fiction and the reality fold in on themselves until both the characters and the reader crave some confirmation of Odysseus' identity. Perhaps his father Laertes can give it, as in Homer's *Odyssey*? But even here Malerba throws doubt into the moment of recognition: whereas, in Homer's *Odyssey*, Odysseus correctly identifies the fruit trees in the orchard and Laertes "recognises the sure signs Odysseus told him" (*Od.* 24.346), here Odysseus mixes the numbers, confusing the apples and the figs. Laertes decides to accept the sign: "Numbers can easily be confused after many years" (p. 120). But neither Telemachus nor the reader are so easily satisfied.

At last, as we approach the novel's end, a form of resolution is reached by which Penelope decides she does not care whether the beggar is Odysseus or not: her *act of recognizing* him will make him Odysseus. "The only certain thing," she says, "is my desperation, because be he the real Odysseus or not, I have recognized him as such, and that's what matters to me. I know that truth and fiction intertwine and become confused, but at this moment, the only man I can welcome into my bed as Odysseus is here in Ithaca" (p. 118). Telemachus, too, decides to welcome Odysseus as his father, thus making him one. "This is his truth," Odysseus comments (p. 126); "this is my truth," he repeats later, as he tells another lying tale to Penelope (p. 133). In the end, it seems, it is the decision that something is true that makes it so: truth is something to be negotiated, constructed, acted out in concert, "supposing that only one truth even exists under the sky" (p. 112).

And this leads us to the final metanarrative twist—the connection between fiction, as both lies and poetry, and its capacity to create and to unravel truth: "Poetry has inside itself a truth that is not of this world, but which comes from the mind of the poet and of the listener" (p. 134). The logical conclusion, of course, is that all this has itself been a fiction—in Malerba's novel, but also in its re-creation as poetry, where Odysseus the master liar now re-creates the game of fiction in the closing pages of *Ithaca Forever* as the self-proclaimed author of the *Iliad* and *Odyssey.* Odysseus the poet and Malerba fuse into one, as manipulators of the limits of fiction and storytellers. But Odysseus has not merely supplanted Malerba. By the end of the tale, Malerba's Odysseus has, in fact, replaced Homer as the creator of the ancient epics—thus supplanting the ancient text, the ancient fiction itself, and revealing the identity beneath the superficial mask of the Homeric *Odyssey* that the novel wears so well.

By the end of *Ithaca Forever,* then, the reader is left in doubt, not only of the truth of the identity of Odysseus and the narrative plot itself—which weaves between recognition and doubt, uncertainty and lies—but also of the relationship of the text itself to the Homeric *Odyssey.* The question of memory, of fidelity, of recognizability in disguise becomes a central theme not only for Odysseus and Penelope but also for the text itself: masked behind the Homeric plot, the troubling and ingenious deception of Malerba's own lying tale lurks always just beneath the surface.

Of course, this sense of disorientation—similar to Odysseus' in landing on the once-familiar Ithaca—is especially pronounced for readers who are coming to *Ithaca Forever* with a fairly detailed knowledge of Homer. Eco notes that "double coding," the possibility of a text "speak[ing] on at least two levels at the same time— that is, it is addressed simultaneously to an élite minority audience using 'high' codes, and to a mass audience using popular codes"[11]—

11. Eco, "Luigi Malerba visto da Eco."

is a common feature of Malerba's citationality. In other words, *Ithaca Forever* can be read on its own as a tale of homecoming, revenge, and disguised identities, or, on another level, as a deconstruction of Homer's *Odyssey*. It is a feature of many modern reworkings of classical texts (including my own) in a world where classical receptions need to appeal to critics (who will often compare a reworking line by line with the original) as well as to popular audiences that may never have had access to the source text. One of the features that makes *Ithaca Forever* such a rewarding read is Malerba's ability to move between Homeric citationality and remarkable inventiveness—keeping his work fresh and accessible for non-Homeric readers.

Emily Hauser
University of Exeter

Ithaca Forever

ODYSSEUS

I've often asked myself how the sea can be salty when the rivers that flow into it and the rain that falls from the sky are not. I've never found the answer, and now, awakened from a deep sleep by the wind, I ask the question anew as I sit here on the rocky shore of this land that I know should be Ithaca, but which I do not recognize.

I look around, confused because I cannot recognize the rocky coast, or the arid land covered by leafless wind-swept trees, or the mountainous horizon, or the sea-blue sky above me. And I wonder where these fragments of porous red rock come from, carried down from the mountains by rushing rains. With every storm, another piece of the world falls into the sea, dragging down dirt and stones, leaving behind holes and naked tree roots. Will the sea someday become one great plain, filled in by the debris of vanished islands and mountains?

Many years ago I hunted for deer and boar in the mountains of my Ithaca, from one peak to another, but I don't remember ever walking over this red sponge-like rock that I find around me, sculpted by the wind and waves. Where does sea salt come from? Where do all these red sponge-like rocks along the shore come from? Where on earth am I? Did the Phaeacian sailors drop me off on the shores of Ithaca, or somewhere else? I've never trusted sailors, whom I know to be the biggest liars in the world.

The difficulties of the war and my long voyage have made me suspicious of everything, so I suspect that the Phaeacian sailors who brought me here waited until I was asleep and then dumped me on the shore of the first deserted island they could find. That way, they could rid themselves of an unwelcome guest once and for all, and steal the gifts that their generous King Alcinous had loaded onto the ship for me. I could see from their anxious faces that they wanted nothing more than to finally sail the high seas in search of their fortune before returning home. But if they had wanted to claim my treasure for themselves, they would have just thrown me overboard into the deep salty sea at night, rather than land on this craggy coast. Maybe they wanted to steal the treasure but didn't want my death on their consciences. Who knows? Fellow feeling sometimes survives even in the hardest of hearts.

But I see something over there, shining underneath the branches at the base of an olive-green shrub at the entrance to a deep cave. There they are, the gold and silver cups and plates that the king of the Phaeacians presented to me before my departure. I'll hide them better with another layer of branches and some heavy stones so that no wanderer can make off with them.

I still don't know if this land is my native Ithaca, or some other little island adrift in the ocean, or simply some unknown coastline. I don't know if this land is inhabited by hospitable men or by giants with a single eye in the middle of their foreheads. I look around, but still don't know if I am home.

I ask myself whether this arid and wild land can be the homeland that I dreamed about for nine long years of war and another ten years of treacherous and adventure-filled voyages. I know that the memory of home can be unreliable indeed. During the years I was away and in times of danger, I imagined my rocky island to be as green and full of flowers as a garden, though in truth it is only good for nourishing the flocks of sheep and goats that graze on dry grasses growing between hard rocks, and for the herds of pigs that grow fat on the acorns that fall in the wooded highlands. I have finally learned that you should never try to make dreams match up with reality.

But I am not telling the whole truth when I say that the years under the walls of Troy were long for me; in truth, they were the fastest years I have ever lived. Hard, happy years. And I can even boast of how I personally was decisive for the victory of the Achaeans. I call it a victory, but who knows if victory is the right word for the destruction of a city and the atrocious events that took place beneath its walls, events that I myself have recounted as moments of glory a hundred times during the stops on my long voyage back.

I left dressed in the robes of the king of Ithaca, and now I'm going to reenter my house dressed in the rags of a beggar that I found in this cave at the edge of the sea, which will allow me to observe secretly—and thus truthfully—what has been going on during my absence. To learn if what I have heard is true, that my house is full of admirers vying for the hand of Penelope, hoping to take my place in my palace and in my bed. How Penelope behaves with these admirers. How Telemachus has grown since I left him behind as a baby. What condition my lands are in. How the servants and handmaidens have been acting in my absence.

Twenty years thrown to the winds? Twenty years without a memorial? Who knows if anyone will ever collect the survivors' stories about the feats of Achilles, Hector of Troy, and Agamemnon of Mycenae, warriors of great heart but limited mind, of their anger and cruelty, and especially of the story of the wooden horse I invented, which allowed us to conquer Troy and return the beautiful Helen to Menelaus of Sparta.

When I think of the struggles, of the wounds, and of the lives lost because of an unfaithful woman like Helen, my mind grows muddled. But when I ignore the cause of the most idiotic war in the world, then I too want its history of events that will never repeat themselves and that have already been consigned to antiquity to be carved in the lasting stone of memory for generations to come.

No woman shall give birth to men like Achilles, Hector, and Agamemnon ever again. The Sparta of Menelaus and the Mycenae of Agamemnon were constructed under the clash of arms and will last as long as the stones with which they were built, which is to say a miserable fraction of eternity. But memory deceives and history is a liar, because men want to remember and listen to fairy tales, not to brutal, stupid reality.

Many things have happened to me in these twenty years, but how many other things must have happened in Ithaca while I was gone? If I can't even recognize my own homeland, which has remained unchanged for centuries, I wonder how much Penelope will have changed, or how I will ever be able to recognize my son Telemachus, no longer a babe in his crib but a full-grown man. How much can a husband and a father who has been so far from his home and his family for all these years count on their love?

And so I'll be on my guard, I'll sneak into my house without being recognized, acting as carefully as my experience tells me to. Who knows if I can depend on Telemachus and on Penelope's devotion, she to whom I have sent my noblest thoughts every day, even amidst the sound of battle and the roar of tempests.

Your children are your children even if they don't know you, even when circumstances make them hate you, but a cheating wife becomes a stranger, unbound to you by relations or blood. I never once doubted Penelope in all these years, so why do questions assail me now, just when I have finally set foot on what I hope are the arid soils of my Ithaca? When the crashing waves threatened my ship, when the winds snapped the strong mainmasts that held my sails aloft, my thoughts flew to Penelope awaiting my return, and the thought of her gave me the strength to fight against all the adversities that jealous gods placed in the way of my homecoming.

Why am I now afraid that I have lost the only reason for my embattled return home? Why now, just when trustfulness would be a warm bed for my exhaustion, do the embittered gods once again resist me and confound my mind with all of these doubts? For years my ears have heard their noisy celebrations high on Olympus after their daily banquets, but I don't hear them anymore, and the bright shell in which I listened to the sound of Penelope's voice was left behind on the ship. The loss of the shell is harder to bear than the loss of the drunken gods' voices. But why should I lament the loss of this shell when soon enough I will be able to listen to Penelope's voice in person?

If I raise my eyes to the sky I can see black hawks with their angular wings, gliding on high as if motionless against that deep blue. If memory doesn't fail, I remember that hawks were rarely seen in the skies above Ithaca. Should I thus think that the farmlands have been left to grow wild and that snakes, the prey of raptors, have taken over?

PENELOPE

I've counted the days, months, and years, and the number overwhelms me. Each morning I have focused my thoughts on my beloved Odysseus, I have recalled our happy days and amorous nights a thousand times, keeping them alive in my memory night after night. In days long gone by I even tried to share his worries, and in the end I forced myself to accept his departure for a war that may have been just for Sparta and Mycenae, but which was unfair to our marriage and without a doubt ruinous for Ithaca.

Troy was so far from our thoughts and from our happy isle, and the war was so foreign to our own interests, that Odysseus would have much preferred to remain behind in his homeland with his family and his adoring subjects. But how could I keep him from leaving for the war when all the other peoples of Hellas were calling his name? I tried to stop him, but his old nurse Eurycleia stood in my way, refusing to give me a hand. It would have been enough to break just his arm or leg with an ax handle. That wouldn't have been so terrible compared to the disaster wrought on us by his departure.

Our small Ithaca had been sailing happily and prosperously on the waters of the ocean, our flocks went out to pasture in the mountains high above the reach of plunderers, and each Suitor peacefully governed his own lands. But when the absence of their king Odysseus grew longer, years longer than expected, they started to show signs of restlessness, taking up residence here in my own house to stuff themselves with food and lay claim to me, expecting me to betray my husband with one of them and prepare myself for another wedding. A curse from the gods fell upon my house, which was transformed into my prison and into a vulgar orgy for my Suitors. I would never be able to betray my conjugal bed, and if I were forced to do so, my admirers would fall upon one another in such competition as to drag Ithaca to its demise.

I've never felt more in need of a strong and courageous man like Odysseus at my side as I do now. My beloved Odysseus, you have been gone too long, and I pray to the gods that my love for you will not turn into anger over your unjustified absence. The Trojan War ended many years ago, but of your return to Ithaca I have heard only unreliable rumors that fly speedily on the wings of Boreas. I have chased from my mind the fear that you perished in a tempestuous storm at sea, and I don't know if I should believe the voices that tell me you are still being held by the Sirens or some Enchantress, or even those who claim that your return to Ithaca is imminent.

My greatest fear, though, more than any Siren or Enchantress, is that you have been entangled in the seductive arts of one of the many depraved women whom the gods throw into the paths of men, and that this is the real reason why you have been gone so long. Even the most steadfast of men can easily fall into temptation. Gossip flutters about my ears, and I have done my best to block it out, relying on all of my faith and my love to do so. I am a weak, lonely woman, but I have known how to turn my bed into an impregnable fortress while you travel in parts unknown throughout the wide world.

I've tricked these gluttonous and haughty Suitors with the story of the shroud that I weave during the day and unravel through the night, but I can feel their suspicions rising, and I fear the guarded whispering amongst them, the knowing grins on their faces.

I know I shouldn't show it, but these years of waiting have eaten away at the lightness of my soul. I cry in my sleep, and when I rise from bed at night to unravel the previous day's work, my pillow is soaked with tears.

ODYSSEUS

The swineherd Eumaios is a rough man, but generous and, most importantly, loyal to his king Odysseus even after a twenty-year absence. I appeared before him dressed as a beggar, a ragged cloak on my back and a satchel hanging from my shoulder, and I force myself to walk bent, supporting my weight with a cane, but I must really look the worse for wear, or perhaps I'm perfectly disguised, if Eumaios didn't recognize me. More than a few times, when I was hunting in this area, he saw me near the pen where he raises pigs, and he also saw me whenever he came to the palace to hand over the animals that were needed for my table. He hasn't recognized me; all the better.

Eumaios invited me into the house where he lives with Galatea, his adolescent daughter, who helps him graze the pigs, prepares his food, and mends his clothes. It is the first time I enter this house. It was considered unseemly for a king to enter the home of a herdsman, and when I had tried to do so I was held back by the men in my retinue. Covered with rags like a beggar, I was kindly welcomed by Eumaios underneath the roof that was forbidden to me when I came dressed as a king.

It is a white stone dwelling plastered with mud and the roof is made of straw, but it is clean, and the fireplace does not seep smoke into the single large room. The floor is of rammed earth and the bed that Eumaios offered me is made of hard stone covered by sheepskins. The house has few furnishings, but enough to cook a fava bean or barley soup and a few hunks of roasted meat. In a large earthenware vase he keeps the olives in brine that we ate before dinner, spitting the seeds into the flames of the fireplace.

I led Eumaios to believe that I am the son of an illustrious prince of Crete, that I fought underneath the walls of Troy for

nine years with Odysseus, and that, after returning to my homeland, I had taken to the sea once again with a small fleet headed
for Egypt in order to begin trading with that country. But there,
I told him, my companions betrayed our agreements and
resorted to common thievery, and it was only thanks to the
intercession of a friendly goddess that my life was saved. I told
how from that distant land I was put on a Phoenician ship to be
sold as a slave. Halfway on our journey to Thessaly, while my
slave drivers stopped along this coast to hunt for some meat and
load fresh water, I managed to slip from the vessel and hide in
the undergrowth.

"So here I am," I said to him, "covered in rags, as you can see,
on this unknown island."

"This is Ithaca, the homeland of Odysseus," Eumaios said.

I had put so much energy into the telling of my tale that I
myself became emotional over my sad destiny as an impover-
ished prince reduced to begging. Poor Eumaios listened to me
with great feeling, and I knew that he would have liked my story
to continue as if it were an exciting tale of adventure, but I told
him that I am no prophet, and that I could not tell him about the
future too.

No one can lie like I can, but even knowing that my stories
were complete inventions, I found myself shamefully sobbing at
the end of them. It is the first time that I have cried so much
since those tears that I vainly tried to hide when Demodocus, in
the palace of the Phaeacians, sang the story of the Trojan horse
in such beautiful verse.

How can this be, this unexpected cloudburst of tears from
the cunning and powerful Odysseus, the sublime liar, the crafty
weaver of deceit? I attributed this strange weakness to the
exhaustion that has tired not my limbs, which remain strong,

but my mind, which is affected by the very words that fall from my lips. I won't blame myself too hard for this, but just as I was unable to hold back my tears earlier, now I cannot hold back my surprise.

Good Eumaios believed my every word, and when I told him that I had been Odysseus' companion under the walls of Troy he embraced me, renewed his offer to host me, and showed great sadness over the long absence of his king. His expressions of loyalty were so sincere that I almost thought he had recognized me, and that his words were guided by well-calculated flattery. But then I understood that the poor herdsman is heartbroken over the fate of this island, which for twenty years has been held up by the fragile shoulders of Penelope, and which has been at risk of descending into chaos and civil war ever since the Suitors from nearby areas have taken up residence in the palace, expecting Penelope to choose Odysseus' successor from among them.

Eumaios called it a civil war, but then said that he wouldn't mind the Suitors slaughtering one another if it weren't for Penelope getting caught in the middle. He has his own ideas about statecraft, this herdsman.

My idea, on the other hand, would be to slip into the palace as a beggar and observe the Suitors' quarrels so as to later intervene with weapons when they are at their most vulnerable. But I obviously cannot act alone, and I don't know if I will be able to keep my head and avoid being recognized when I am next to Penelope. And Penelope, whom Eumaios declares has been faithful to Odysseus, how is she behaving with these admirers? What does she concede to these princely usurpers to keep them at bay?

I asked Eumaios many questions, since he often goes to the palace to bring animals to be slaughtered for the Suitors' banquets. Has he seen Penelope in their company? Who does she seem to like the most?

"It's impossible," I said to him, "that a beautiful young woman like Penelope has been able to hold them back without offering anything in return. Who amongst all the Suitors do you think is her favorite?"

"How do you, foreigner, know that Penelope is young and beautiful?"

"Odysseus talked to me about her many times. The men always spoke much about their women during the lulls in the fighting."

Eumaios is a simple soul and incapable of casting doubt on the queen he adores as much as an Olympian goddess, as he put it.

"But even the Olympian goddesses," I rebutted, "have their favorites, and they often take great liberties, just like prostitutes."

Eumaios took offense at these words and scolded me, waving his arms and raising his voice.

"I'll make you march right out of this house if you're not careful. What terrible thing have my ears heard from the mouth of a foreigner whom I have received in my house? How dare you speak of prostitutes and throw such slander on Queen Penelope?"

"Perhaps I let my tongue get carried away and I offended the goddesses of Olympus," I said, "but I never wanted to offend Penelope."

"I know that Antinous is chief among the Suitors," Eumaios revealed to me, "but this does not mean that Penelope has chosen him. I know that her admirers have argued furiously and that Antinous, the best among them for courage and beauty, has been able to position himself ahead of them all. I know nothing else, and even the things I am telling you, O foreigner, are just rumors garnered from the palace handmaidens, gossipy women who hate one another as much as Penelope's admirers do."

"How many of these admirers are there, though?"

"I know that there are so many they have filled the palace, but I have never counted them."

"Ten? Fifty?"

"I count my pigs every day, but I have never counted Penelope's admirers. I think it must be closer to fifty than ten."

I have understood that I could never fight all those young Suitors, and that I should study their strengths before facing them with weapons. I'm still hoping the gods and fate will not fail me.

PENELOPE

I have already held out against the siege of the Suitors longer than Troy against the siege of the Achaeans, but time neglects the plans, the thoughts, and the feelings of a woman who has no walls or weapons in her defense as Helen did. I have survived these months and years without surrendering, and I have measured my private war against that distant one which the besieged Trojans fought, and I still hope that one day Odysseus will arrive and invent a new horse to free me. This would be a just cause, better than fighting for that adulterous Helen, whom Odysseus had wisely refused as his wife, who provoked an atrocious war and thousands of deaths and a destroyed city because of her running off with the youthful Paris.

Time does not flow equally in all places, the days and years of the siege of Troy are not the same as the days and years of my solitude here in Ithaca. And the ten years that have passed for me and for Odysseus since the war ended? Who has lost them? Who has gained them?

It is true that I have held out longer than the Trojans, but the Suitors continue their assault, intent on sapping my energy and eating my bread until I become a solitary, naked prey. The gods rarely concede the privilege of being able to fill the space between one day and another, one year and another, with hope. Poor Queen Penelope, where is your crown? How much pain, how much sadness, how many sleepless nights still await you?

Last night I dreamt I was wearing a burnished iron cuirass and gripping a sword that was so large and heavy that it dragged my arm to the ground. Thus armed, I entered the hall where the Suitors were banqueting noisily, with coarse singing. When they saw me, they fell silent in terror, and the moment I lifted the sword in a threatening manner they fled, and the palace quickly became deserted.

I don't know what message the gods were trying to send me in this dream, whether it is a truthful proclamation coming through the gate of horn, or a false promise passing through the gate of ivory. But why search for obscure meanings in such a clear dream? I want only to know what import a nocturnal desire can have for my unhappy life. A prodding? To do what? Is there anything I can do? No advice from any quarter. The sky is mute and the gods distant. What am I saying—it is the sky that is distant and the gods mute.

Dreams are like the cries of the seagulls that I interpret as good or bad omens based on how I feel. These days, the gulls sound like frightened voices, as if something terrible were to happen, but I know that this is true only in my distraught imagination, and that I should not listen to these stupid sea birds that make such a racket over my head for no reason.

ODYSSEUS

Every morning Eumaios brings two pots of boiled turnips mixed with the residue from the olive press to the sows who are suckling their piglets. He brought me to see a sow that cannot suckle all thirteen piglets that she had just given birth to, because she only has twelve teats. The twelve little pigs, each of which has laid claim to its own teat, will allow no one else to suck milk from their mother. The thirteenth, left out, is being fed by Eumaios with goat's milk until he is able to eat by himself.

"Thirteen is a bad number and I don't know if we will be able to save him," said Eumaios, who believes in the magic of numbers.

"In that case, let me tell you that on the island of the Phaeacians there reign thirteen kings and the thirteenth, Alcinous, is the richest and most powerful of them all. And when Odysseus was shipwrecked off the coast of the Phaeacian island, his twelve sailors were swallowed by the waves and he, the thirteenth, was saved."

Eumaios looked at me suspiciously.

"How do you know these things about Odysseus? You certainly couldn't have spoken about his shipwreck while under the walls of Troy."

"Merchants ply the seas and land in ports. They are the ones who bring the news."

I accompanied the herdsman from the sows' pen to that of the other pigs, which he released and led, along with Galatea, to forage in the oak woods. I saw that he would have been disappointed if I had not joined them. The herdsman explained that twice a year, in spring and fall, he has to clear the underwood of brambles so that the pigs can feed more easily on the acorns that fall from the oak and beech trees. In addition to Galatea, he has two boys who work for him in the glades, collecting chests of acorns that will be stored for winter.

The pigs grunted contentedly as they rooted through the dry leaves, then lifted their heads to chew the acorns found on the ground.

Every time he takes the animals to pasture, Eumaios brings a bow and a quiver of arrows to hunt wild rabbits.

"When I bring the animals down to the Suitors, all they leave me is the head, and sometimes only the ears and tail. And so I try to catch some wild rabbits, which Galatea roasts on a spit or stews in wine for me."

At one point, while we were walking through a clearing, I saw a flock of wild ducks coming. I quickly grabbed the bow from Eumaios' hands, and when the ducks were overhead, I let an arrow fly. With a single shot, I brought down a good-sized duck, which I gathered and handed over to Galatea.

Eumaios was speechless for the speed and accuracy of my shot, and he stared with wide eyes of amazement.

"Never seen anyone shoot so well," he said.

"I started practicing archery when I was a boy, and I obviously got a lot of practice during the Trojan War," I told him.

"I'm not bad with a bow myself, but I've never hit a flying duck. Only Odysseus could do that."

I'll have to be more careful, otherwise Eumaios will become suspicious. I handed over the bow and arrows, and we continued walking in the burning sun, past a small garden where Eumaios was growing turnips.

"Those turnips are also for the winter. They're good for the pigs, but when they are roasted over embers and seasoned with the oil that this island so abundantly produces and a pinch of salt, they're good for men too."

We got home at sunset, passing by a spring where the pigs sated their thirst. Eumaios washed the wheels of the cart that he uses to bring the pigs into town, then we went inside, sat down in front of the fire, and ate barley soup cooked by Galatea, then the duck, roasted with watercress, veronica, and seaweed on a spit, along with small flatbreads cooked on a hot stone. And we washed our dinner down with a glass of red wine, flavored with resin.

After dinner, I listened patiently as the good herdsman told me about his life, his early days with his father, a lord from the island of Syros, about his abduction by a band of Phoenician marauders, and of his being sold to Laertes, the king of Ithaca, which has since become his beloved homeland. Landed in Ithaca, his story carried on until late, when sleep made our eyelids heavy and our heads droop.

Out of the many words I heard between wakefulness and sleep, I learned that Telemachus, trying to uncover news about me, faced the dangers of a long sea voyage, arriving in Pylos in Messenia to ask the elderly Nestor for news, and then in Sparta, where Menelaus lived with Helen, reinstated to her conjugal bed after the fall of Troy.

Eumaios was told by a traveling merchant that Telemachus left Sparta two weeks ago and should have returned by now. He looked worried, though, about his arrival because he fears the Suitors have set some sort of trap.

I have thus arrived in Ithaca in time to watch over my son's fate. I decided that I will go into town as soon as possible, dressed once again as a beggar, so as to keep Telemachus from being betrayed by the Suitors in an ambush. They can hardly bear the presence of Odysseus' son, his legitimate heir, on the island.

"Of course," Eumaios said, "it is a real stroke of bad luck that Odysseus is far from Ithaca in a moment of danger. He has either been shipwrecked by a storm or become an adventurer, because the war in Troy has been over for ten years now. I've heard that some soldiers, rather than return home, have turned to the life of outlaws."

"Is that what you think of your king?"

"What are you saying? I was talking about soldiers who don't want to go back to their wives. Odysseus is a king and has a beautiful and honest wife whom he loved."

He sat in silence, then offered a private reflection.

"I think war changes the way men think."

"There are men, though, that are born for war," I said. "Achilles, Agamemnon, Hector, Ajax were heroes with a sword and spear, and Odysseus was no less; I remember that he handled his weapons no less adroitly than them, but he was different. Odysseus was a man of stratagems, and he told everyone who would listen that future wars would not be won by brute force but by strategy and cunning above all. He even said that the age of the sword and spear was finished, and that an age of numbers and words was coming."

Eumaios looked at me, his face showing confusion.

"What did he mean? Before leaving Ithaca, Odysseus was a champion archer, but I don't know if he philosophized about numbers and words. It is true that he enjoyed telling stories, and he always found the right words to make people listen."

"Under the walls of Troy, everyone stopped to listen to his tales," I said.

"The legend of his deeds has traveled all the way to Ithaca, and everyone says that Troy fell when that wooden horse with its belly full of soldiers invented by Odysseus entered within the walls. But what does all of this matter if first the war and then the return voyage have kept him far from Penelope and his son Telemachus, who are now in grave danger?"

"So you have heard news about a plot against Telemachus?"

"The herald Medon fears that terrible things will happen when Telemachus reappears in the palace after his trip to Sparta. Telemachus is very young and will do something careless. All of our troubles began with that pointless war that took our king from Ithaca and put the island's sovereignty at risk. What did we care if they had stolen Menelaus' wife? Stolen? Rumors say that Helen ran off willingly with Paris. And Menelaus decided to drag all of the Achaeans into a war over a bedroom affair."

"In fact, only Agamemnon, king of the Mycenaeans and brother of Menelaus, immediately accepted the invitation to go off to war. The other Achaeans had no intention of getting their ships and men involved in such a distant war."

"Even Odysseus did what he could, using words and tricks, to avoid going, but Troy must have been written in his destiny."

"Not even Achilles, the heroic Achilles, wanted to leave for Troy," I said. "His parents had sent him to Skyros in the court of King Lycomedes, where he disguised himself as a woman. It was Odysseus himself, once he had joined up with the other Achaeans, who discovered the trick and exposed him. He presented himself at Lycomedes' court disguised as a merchant and showed his goods to the women, sliding weapons in amid the jewels, fabric, and silk ribbons. Young Achilles immediately showed his interest in the weapons, ignoring all the rest, whereupon everyone understood who he was. Dropping the disguise, he was easily convinced by Odysseus to sail with the others. This story was whispered under the walls of Troy, but Achilles never said a single word about it to anyone, and no one dared speak about it with him."

"Maybe it's an undignified story for a hero," Eumaios said, "but I think Achilles was a hundred times right to hide himself, since he lost his life in Troy."

PENELOPE

Should I perhaps thank the gods that Telemachus resembles his father Odysseus? It's just like men to say nothing of their plans, or even their thoughts, to women. Be they wives or mothers, women are never worthy of their secrets.

So one fine day Odysseus left for the war in Troy, leaving behind Telemachus in diapers; and, like him, Telemachus sailed in secret to Pylos and Sparta, where he hoped to learn something about his father from Nestor and Menelaus. Would I have forbidden it if he had spoken to me? Certainly not. So why then have me hear about his departure from the old nurse Eurycleia after he was already sailing toward Peloponnesus?

Odysseus, in truth, could not have avoided his departure, even though he would have preferred to stay in his homeland, shooting arrows at wild boars rather than Trojans. And I was unable to keep him from going. But then every story we hear tells of how he fought like a hero and that Troy fell because of that wooden horse pulled inside the city, thanks to his cunning and genius. It is for this that I worry, that his experiences during the war have given too much satisfaction to his vanity and pride. How else can you explain these infinite delays on his return voyage, if not for the fear that a peaceful life as king of Ithaca, next to his wife, his son, and his friends, would not be enough for his ambitions of glory?

I'll never tell anyone about these thoughts of mine, and I will forget them the day that, thanks to some divine intervention, Odysseus appears at the palace gate. In the meantime, friends have become enemies and servants traitors, but hope has never left me, and I myself have learned how to conspire, just like Odysseus, and I await, eyes fixed on the horizon, my moment of revenge, as a reward for my patience.

Telemachus, as he left behind his adolescent years, already seemed to be no less restless than his father, equally deceitful, untrusting, and gripped by insatiable curiosity. But in the name of the gods, how could he have thought that I would forbid him to seek news of his father? Faithful Eurycleia told me today that Antinous, the strongest and quickest-tempered of the Suitors, is scheming against him, and this makes me think that Telemachus is already on his way back. But I hope Eurycleia is wrong, for Antinous knows that any offense to Telemachus would be like an offense to myself, and this will not serve his purposes. In fact he always showed a hypocritical affection for Telemachus as a boy, one day even making him a present of a small ash-wood bow with a set of arrows and a leather quiver. Eurycleia sees conspiracies everywhere; maybe she is overly suspicious, but I should nevertheless keep my eyes wide open, even against the old nurse's nightmares.

I have too many troubles to confront day after day without a man's help, and now it is I who will have to protect Telemachus. I know very well that a sword does not befit my arms, and I envy those who can fight their enemies with weapons, even if their lives are at risk. It must be an inconceivable pleasure to bring your enemy down with your sword. Unhappy human who is forced to suffer constantly and impotently in solitude. I know that I must find within myself, not in weapons that I cannot use, nor in the gods of Olympus who do not listen to my prayers, the strength to face this insolent and raucous horde.

My thoughts run constantly toward Odysseus, with regrets and unexpected disappointments. His departure for the Trojan War was a disaster for me, but I can't blame Odysseus, who staked his own dignity in an attempt to keep away from that senseless undertaking. The full strength of the Achaeans was recruited, from every city and every island in Greece, and they said at the time that the war would last no longer than a year. A prediction that helped me bear Odysseus' departure without many tears, but then things went well past that prediction because of the tenacity of the besieged, the heroics of Hector and his companions, and the unkindness of fate. Not one, but nine years of war.

Many of the warriors who fought beneath those walls have long since returned to their homes, sleep in their beds with their wives, sit at meals with their children, manage their affairs. Others received a tragic welcome in their homelands, like Agamemnon, rightfully punished by Fate for having sacrificed his daughter Iphigenia at the moment of his departure so as to gain a favorable wind for sailing. Only Odysseus is still missing, and when I try to control the rage that rises from my guts and disturbs my sleep it is only because I fear that he has been swept away by tempestuous seas and that the dark realms of Hades have welcomed him.

The mournful cries of the seagulls unsettle my solitude and bring sad thoughts. I will not go downstairs to the large hall today where the Suitors feast and get drunk while the singer Terpiade tries to cover their disgusting noises with his cithara and his voice.

ODYSSEUS

I had trouble finding sleep on the bed that good Eumaios offered me, and I awoke more than once during the night and stayed awake for a long while. My fortitude, so strong in the past, all of a sudden seems to melt like wax in a fire. What obscure illness is this, gods of Olympus?

Telemachus arrived by sea this morning and, before heading to the city and the palace, chose to come here to loyal Eumaios and ask him to bring the news of his return to Penelope.

I observed him in amazement, and with strong emotions. I would not have recognized him if Eumaios had not told me that this was Odysseus' son. He is a tall, thin boy, and I would say he resembles Penelope quite a bit. His eyes are blue like his mother's, though his face is broad like mine and he has a strange smile from I don't know who. Maybe my elderly father Laertes smiles like him.

I had to keep my emotions in check before revealing myself, I didn't want to show myself with tears in my eyes to a son who knows nothing more about me than the legend of my deeds. Why must I constantly hold back this shameful rain of tears that falls from my eyes at the worst possible moments, now that I tread the warm ground of my homeland? My arms are still powerful and I know I can be fearsome with a sword and bow, but my soul is fragile and breaks down at the touch of any emotion.

When Eumaios took the pigs to forage, I pulled Telemachus, who had from the very beginning looked at me suspiciously, toward me and slowly began to speak about the siege of Troy, my return voyage, and my stay on the island of the Phaeacians. While I spoke, his interest grew, and when he heard about the Phaeacians he asked me immediately if I had met Odysseus on that island.

"Certainly," I answered him, "we came here to Ithaca on the same ship, and you now have Odysseus, your father, before your eyes disguised as a beggar."

Telemachus looked at me, confused. He could not believe that his illustrious father Odysseus was hiding under these beggar's rags, he whose feats had echoed throughout every part of this vast world. He still watched me, incredulous, but when I described the entire palace and his nursery room and the room of his parents and the small room where my bow was kept, and even the bronze lion-shaped andirons in the fireplace and the awning over the wood for the winter and then asked if the nursemaid Eurycleia was still alive and if she still ate a slice of bread with honey every morning, Telemachus embraced me, crying.

"I'm sorry I didn't recognize you, but when you left Ithaca I was very young and I can't remember you. But why didn't even the herdsman recognize you?"

"I am disguised as a beggar precisely so as not to be recognized. And after all, Eumaios was less than twenty years old when I left, and he had only seen me during hunting trips in this area. Just a few times."

I explained to Telemachus that for the moment, only he could know who I was, because I wanted to slip into the palace and study a plan of attack together with him before confronting the Suitors. This was the reason for the beggar's disguise.

Pleased by the conspiratorial trust that I placed in him, Telemachus told me that one time, Antinous had invited him to a hunting party, but that the host had shot badly, and instead of striking a deer, the arrow had grazed his throat. And he showed me a slight scar on his neck.

"Since then, I trust neither Antinous nor any of the other Suitors."

"They will try to kill you again, but we will use a surprise attack and slaughter them."

"A difficult challenge, but perhaps not impossible for one whose cunning brought down the city of Troy," Telemachus said proudly. "The Suitors are young and handle weapons well, they have come from Same, from Dulichium, from Zakynthos, and from Ithaca itself, and they will fight tooth and nail to protect the privileges they have attained through their insolence. But they have gotten soft from all the food and wine, and this makes them more vulnerable."

"Loyal Eumaios," I told Telemachus, "will go straight to the palace as you decided and announce your arrival to Penelope. No more than this, for not even your mother can know that Odysseus is hidden beneath the clothes of this vagabond. Not Eumaios either, naturally, for despite the warm welcome he gave me in his house, he could let slip some clue to Penelope or the handmaidens. I want it to be me alone, disguised as I am and allowed into the palace on your authority, who watches with my own eyes the state of things and prepares, with you, a scheme for defeating the Suitors. As far as Penelope is concerned, I want to be convinced of her faithfulness myself. I trust nothing as much as my own eyes, and in a single glance I will understand both the things that can be seen and those that are concealed. I, then, will decide the right moment to reveal myself."

"Penelope hates her admirers and her disdain for them is as high as a mountaintop. But I can understand why you might prefer not to show yourself even to her. If this is what you have decided, I agree."

I see that the story of the Trojan horse is recounted as a great tale of adventure and has spread my fame to the four corners of the earth. I fought and risked my life a hundred times, I led desperate battles and escaped unharmed, but I have become the man of the Trojan horse, even to Telemachus. He repeated that if Troy was conquered in the end because of me, he was sure I would also invent some clever contraption to rout the raving Suitors who were trying to remove our family from governing Ithaca.

"With cunning and luck," I said, "we'll send them all to warm the earth. And remember that good fortune does not fall from the sky, but is a virtue. I have always depended on my good fortune, more than bravery and cunning, and it has never yet abandoned me in my moments of danger."

PENELOPE

Eumaios arrived midmorning with two pigs for the Suitors' feast. He sent a handmaiden to my room because he wanted to tell me something. Good news.

"Telemachus has arrived," he told me, "and today will come to you here in the palace. I am happy too, my queen, and hope you will allow me to drink a large cup of wine this evening in celebration of the return of Odysseus' son."

"Telemachus is my son too," I replied.

I was waiting for Telemachus' return and now I fear for his life. The Suitors are at a fever pitch and will not look kindly on his presence within the palace. Odysseus' son will be a cause of embarrassment for them, and if they had not feared losing my tolerance of them definitively, they would have already killed him. And how can Telemachus continue to put up with these men who want to take his father's place?

I have learned to live slowly, I have ruined my eyes and fingers weaving and unraveling the burial shroud for Laertes on the loom, I have examined the sky every single day to find some favorable omen, but the sky and the Olympian gods are unconcerned about my desires.

Many times I have controlled my wrath toward the Suitors, but for how much longer will I be able to hide my feelings behind this curtain of fictions between day and night? The seagulls, lords of the light, screech above me, they glide through the air in front of my eyes and seem to want to tell me something. I cannot speak their language, but if they can read my heart they must be very sorry for me.

ODYSSEUS

While I was approaching the palace with Telemachus and loyal Eumaios, we were assaulted along the way by bloody insults from a certain Melanthius, a goatherd in the pay of the Suitors.

"Where are you taking this tramp? This repugnant bum? Are you headed for the palace to stuff him with table scraps? You should have him sweep the dunghill, he deserves no better."

As he spoke, Melanthius stuck out his foot and kicked me. I became black with rage, but I kept myself from smashing his head so as not to carelessly jeopardize my agreed-upon plan with Telemachus.

Ithaca is unrecognizable. I could never have imagined my city falling into such a state of abandon. There is an efflorescence on the façades of buildings that makes them look leprous, the stones on the streets have become separated, and tufts of weeds that no one bothers tearing out are growing in the cracks. Gusts of wind raise clouds of dust and dry leaves. The palaestra has been completely abandoned and a large wild fig tree is growing in the middle of it.

Just outside the palace gates, along the outer wall, there was a pile of animal bones with strips of meat still hanging from them, bloody skins, piles of rotten vegetables, all the scraps from the banquets.

An old dog that lived near these scraps, his source of food, began wagging his tail the moment he saw me, dragged himself to his feet, and came toward me. I recognized him immediately, my poor dog Argos. He too has waited many years for me and is now so thin that his bones are barely covered by his skin, not from lack of food but from implacable old age. My poor loyal dog Argos, if men were as loyal as you and the herdsman Eumaios, my return would be truly tranquil and happy. But instead, here I am, covered with rags and a scraggly beard, and I have to struggle to walk with my back bent over, supporting myself with a cane so as not to be recognized.

Again I had to hold back my tears when my dog Argos fell to the ground and I knew that he would never stand up again, killed by the emotion of seeing his master after so many years. I stretched my hand out to give him a pat on the head; he opened his eyes for a moment, and then closed them again in the darkness of death. How many runs did we take together through the thick vegetation while chasing wild boars, and how happy we were when we had a good hunt, my poor dog Argos.

Welcomed with dignity by a poor swineherd who lives in the mountains, kicked in the streets by a vile goatherd, and remembered with love by the decrepit old dog Argos, who could not bear the strain, this is how the heroic Odysseus has been welcomed by his realm after a bloody war and adventure-filled voyage home. Where are the festive standards and the joyous songs sung by his subjects, where are the garlands of flowers that are given to victors upon their return to their homeland? Where is his wife, where her gentle touch? Not only my eyes but my heart cries too under these beggar's rags.

I followed Telemachus and Eumaios into the great hall of the palace, leaning on my cane like an old man in need of food and rest, and I stopped at the doorway as is proper for one who lives on charity.

The Suitors were feasting to the sounds of the singer Terpiade and hardly noticed our entrance. Antinous alone waved a greeting to Telemachus and raised a cup of wine in his direction. A few of the other Suitors gave the slightest of nods to Telemachus, as if he were just an ordinary guest and not the heir to the throne.

Telemachus told Eumaios to give me a loaf of bread, which I placed in my satchel, and then invited me to ask the Suitors for a handout as soon as Terpiade finished his song.

At this, Antinous upbraided Eumaios.

"Why have you brought yet another freeloader into the city when we are already infested by an army of scrap-eating bums? We know you complain every single time we ask you to slaughter your pigs for our meals, and now, with no shame, you want to add another ravenous mouth to those that already hound us at all hours?"

Eumaios answered Antinous by saying that singers, or master artisans, or healers, not to mention tricksters boxers toadies charlatans and good-for-nothings of every variety are welcomed in the palace and laden with gifts, but when a beggar in need arrives, no one feels any sorrow for him.

Encouraged by Eumaios' words, I too turned to Antinous so as to test his arrogance.

"You," I said, "certainly wouldn't even give salt to a poor hungry beggar who entered your own house if you don't have the kindness to give me a piece of bread that is not even yours."

Then the haughty Antinous, feeling himself under accusation for eating another person's bread, grabbed a stool and hit me from behind with it. Once again I had to hold myself back, clenching my teeth, knowing full well that Antinous, among all the Suitors, was the most powerful and considered by all to be the first among Penelope's admirers. I rolled to the ground as if the blow had shattered my shoulder bones, causing the Suitors to laugh riotously. As if a man's pain was a jolly spectacle. But to them, I am a beggar, not a man.

All this took place while Penelope wisely remained alone in her rooms on the upper floor.

How I will be able to put up with this agonizing pretense, I can't say. It is quite another thing to fight face-to-face against an enemy, or design an ingenious horse with its belly full of soldiers under the walls of Troy. Here, Odysseus is no longer Odysseus. I have been kicked by a vile goatherd and then struck on the shoulder by Antinous. He will be the first to die when the time comes for revenge.

I have not seen Penelope yet. But how disturbing is my return, how much humiliation and how many insults. If I had not been rewarded by the joy of meeting Telemachus, and if I had not had the consolation of the loyalty of the herdsman Eumaios and my poor dog Argos, I would not know on which god to call in order to find the strength to bear such a welcoming.

Telemachus was also able to control his anger when I was hit by Antinous. He showed only what he thought was the right amount of concern for a poor beggar who had arrived at the palace door in his company. A few words in my defense, but not a movement or a look that betrayed the truth.

Telemachus went upstairs to greet his mother while I waited downstairs on the threshold of the great hall. He was gone a long time in Penelope's rooms, but I am sure he revealed nothing about my arrival, as we agreed. He knows perfectly well that one should never trust women, and I think he is learning how to interpret the ways of the world or, rather, the ways of this little world in the middle of the vast ocean in which our lives are circumscribed. Beyond the palace, distant cities, countrysides, forests, the infinite sea, rivers, caverns and wild animals, flowered gardens. At the moment, Ithaca is just a prison, nothing belongs to me here anymore, and I have to regain my kingdom and my patient prisoner wife by force, with cunning and luck. I tell myself a hundred times that I am not Odysseus but a beggar covered in rags who suffers his insults in silence.

When Telemachus came down from the upper rooms, his eyes were as red as fire. He tried to hide his face so I would not see, but it was obvious that he and his mother had cried for a long time together. For heaven's sake! there is constant crying everywhere I look, and I can't take this sea of tears anymore.

What misfortune that I too have been stricken by this malady. The slightest emotion and I immediately feel my eyes swelling like clouds before the rain, and when I am unable to stop the tears I am infinitely ashamed. I ask again, is it because of the exhaustion that built up during my long voyage home? Is it a sign of sadness, or of liberation from mistakes in the past?

Telemachus told me that Penelope is worried, but that she still has her full beauty despite the melancholy and suffering that have been her constant companions, that she still dresses elegantly, that she soaks her long black hair in a nettle infusion every day. He told me no more, and I asked no questions.

PENELOPE

The Suitors' arrogance and the smoke from the roasted meat that they devour like hungry wolves every day has poisoned the air and made it choking. The palace walls are steeped in the stench of food from banquets. These admirers of mine act as if they had gone hungry in their own homes and now wanted to gorge themselves in Odysseus' house and at his expense. They hope he is dead, they want him dead, but nevertheless a misgiving remains in their souls because no certain news of him has arrived on the island. Odysseus' ghost makes them irritable and rowdy.

I too have little hope to see Odysseus return, even if Telemachus brings—aside from rumors about the difficulties of his voyage and his imprisonment on the island of Circe—news that he may have invented to make me feel better, news that Odysseus is already sailing the seas toward Ithaca from the island of the Phaeacians.

Whenever I close my eyes, no matter the time of day, I see his ship sailing across the waves of the sea, and it doesn't require much imagination to know that he is coming toward Ithaca. Sometimes I hear the whistling of the wind and the crash of the waves against the black hull of the ship and Odysseus' voice giving orders to the sailors. But this image has pointlessly comforted me and upset me for too many years now.

The thought of Odysseus follows me everywhere, on those rare walks with my faithful Eurycleia by the sea and on the dusty roads of Ithaca, in the gardens and orchards around the city where I go every autumn when it is time to harvest fruit for the winter and grapes for making wine. When I visit the olive press where they crush the olives and fill the amphorae with green, pungent oil, I always see Odysseus walking beside me like a shadow. When I visit the grottoes where the wine is made and stored, the farmers always ask me to taste the must, which I do not like, and every time I have to give them my encouragement and compliments for the fruits of their labor, as Odysseus would do.

The farmers are pleased by these visits and will later speak about them for many days. They observe my clothes, count the wrinkles on my face, and remember and repeat my words. I am their queen and I cannot remain forever ensconced in my rooms; I have to let my subjects see me, exchange a few words with them, offer small gifts.

One time I even went up the mountain where the swineherd Eumaios, whom I see occasionally when he brings animals for the feasts, welcomed me with tears. He wouldn't dare speak to me, but I learned from the nurse Eurycleia that he has remained loyal to his king and hates the Suitors who devour the animals that he raises with such care. Animals that are raised on the island belong to Odysseus and, during his absence, belong to me and Telemachus, but they butcher animals large and small every day without paying a single coin. I spoke about this one day with Ctesippus, the richest of them all, who replied that he plans on paying his debts, and that we will settle up one day. One day when?

During the long evenings passed in loneliness, while the scent of olive or cypress wood spreads throughout the palace from the fireplace and rises to my rooms, I feel the sudden need to speak about Odysseus, but I don't know to whom. And so I pronounce his name all night long like a madwoman. But I am not crazy; I may be desperate, but I am not crazy. Madness is a luxury that I cannot afford.

Now this vagabond has arrived who claims to have been at Odysseus' side under the walls of Troy and who, having himself journeyed far and wide along the sea and earth, has perhaps gathered recent news. So says the good Eumaios, who hosted him in his mountainside home.

I was unsure whether to bring this vagabond here to my rooms so as to hear in secret what he has to say about Odysseus, but Eurycleia argued against it, first of all because it is not proper for a queen to accept a beggar in her rooms and second because she fears that he is only telling clever lies in order to find hospitality.

"That's the usual way with these vagabonds who pretend to know the past and future or who put on a show with games and riddles," the old nurse said, "in order to scrounge a bit from one person and a bit from another."

"As opposed to the Suitors," I said to her, "who scrounge off of Penelope alone."

I don't understand Telemachus. Why on earth, after having just landed on the island, does he offer his protection and friendship to the first vagabond he meets on the road? Strange and careless behavior, not becoming of the son of the mistrustful and cunning king of Ithaca. If this vagabond is truly of noble origin and a hostile fate has reduced him to this state of ruin, as he told both Eumaios and Telemachus, only in that case does he deserve our attention, for he may have visited places and met people we are interested in.

Eurycleia insists that it is not appropriate to allow a beggar into my rooms, but before whom must I feel restraint? Certainly not before Antinous, who, they tell me, struck the poor man, failing to respect the sacred law of hospitality. But what am I saying? Do I already think of Antinous as the master of my house? It can only be my great tiredness that makes me expect the most violent and arrogant of my admirers to uphold duties of hospitality that are not his. In this manner, I am offending myself and my dignity, the memory of Odysseus, Telemachus' authority, and the benevolent spirits that have helped me over these years. No, Antinous has no duties of hospitality; this is not and shall never be his house.

I took Eurycleia's advice. I will meet this vagabond in the great hall, but not in front of the Suitors. If he has any news, let it be for me, and not for them.

Many things are changing these days under the skies of Ithaca. The horizon seems to have suddenly expanded beyond the palace walls and my gaze loses itself in the distance, hoping to spy a friendly light. Telemachus has arrived from his voyage of exploration and says that Odysseus is alive in some corner of the sea. According to other rumors, so ephemeral that they seem to have been carried here by the wind, Odysseus has set sail from the island of the Phaeacians, where he was an honored guest, and has returned to the sea in the direction of Ithaca.

But what if he has fallen in love with Nausicaa, daughter of the king of the Phaeacians, as a Phoenician trader has told? Or is it not more likely that Nausicaa has fallen in love with him? A disaster in either case.

The stories about the siege of Troy have kept our souls anxious for many years, but still no one has brought me realistic news about Odysseus' return, only fables about Sirens, Sorceresses, and Sea Monsters that you might tell around the evening fire. So let's hear the words of this old man come to Ithaca from far-off lands. If he gives me good, honest news I will not hesitate to give him expensive gifts, new clothes, and whatever else he desires. But if I perceive that he is weaving pleasant stories just to appease me and receive my hospitality and gifts, as Eurycleia suspects, well, I will send him away harshly so that no one ever thinks to make fun of my grief.

Never more than now, now that Telemachus is back in Ithaca, have I wished for Odysseus' return and his revenge against these insatiable admirers who slaughter oxen and pigs every day, making the smoke of the singed meat on the spits rise all the way to the sky, and drinking all of the wine stored in our grottoes.

My repugnance for Antinous, who seems to have been nominated the leader among all the admirers, has nothing to do with his physical aspect, which I have to admit is pleasing, but comes from his arrogant and violent behavior. One night when I was awakened by wild noises that came from down below, I stood on my toes and peered over the stairs and saw him dancing drunkenly and totally naked in the middle of the great hall, to the approval of all the others. A naked man dancing is a disgusting sight.

ODYSSEUS

I asked Telemachus to arrange my meeting with Penelope in a way that it would not be witnessed by the Suitors, sometime after sunset when all of them, along with the naked and masked handmaidens, would have left for the Dionysian festival held every changing moon in the abandoned palaestra. Who knows how many rumors the Suitors would spread if they saw such a rattletrap beggar called in to speak with the queen. Telemachus' arrival has already put them on edge, and I saw that when he arrived in the hall they welcomed him coldly, almost like a stranger, and whispered amongst themselves and exchanged knowing glances.

But another reason led me to make this request, and this is because the half-light of the lamps will not betray me. As well disguised as I am under the clothes of a beggar and as good as I am in faking old age despite my years, I would not want Penelope to recognize me or harbor any suspicions. Women are always alert in any circumstance, but when they have a man in front of them, be he old or young, rich or poor, their gaze goes right through him and they can even read the secrets of his soul. Women are fearsome and Penelope, despite her show of ingenuousness, is more fearsome than others.

Unfortunately, something happened that made me break my promise to submit to any provocation in silence so as to avoid creating suspicion about my identity. A beggar named Iros, who lords it over everyone in the streets and neighborhoods of the city and who has won the right to beg within the palace, thought that his prestige as top beggar in Ithaca was under attack when he saw my satchel full of the food scraps that I had gotten from the Suitors.

"Beat it, you filthy old man," he said upon seeing me seated in the palace atrium, "if you don't want me to drag you out of here by your feet. By the consent of my generous protectors, only I can stay here in this atrium."

"In this atrium," I replied, "there is room for both of us without stepping on each other's toes. But if you keep it up with your insults and threats, I will beat you to a pulp and make your flabby, disgusting body bleed, even if I am older than you."

The Suitors, already wearing masks for the Dionysian orgy, spurred us to quarrel, hoping for a free show of fists, quite sure that their own vagabond would beat me easily.

Encouraged by the shouts of the Suitors, the vagabond continued to insult me, never imagining that it was Odysseus himself under my rags.

"I'll pound you with my two hands," the repugnant Iros threatened once again, "and I'll make your whole set of teeth go flying. And so, if you're brave enough to take on a younger, stronger man than yourself, come closer and hit me, if you can."

Among the Suitors, Antinous was the most excited, already anticipating a good show.

"This is a rare opportunity we're about to have here before our very eyes," he said loudly to get everyone's attention, "a show that not even the mimes in the theater are capable of putting on."

At his words, all of the Suitors formed a circle and urged us on with their voices and gestures.

The beggar raised his hands in a fighting stance and I also made a move toward him, throwing the rags that covered my body to the ground. Iros had a moment of panic when he saw that I was more robust and muscular than he had imagined in his wretched mind. He took a step forward and punched me in the shoulder. In return, I hit him with a sharp blow under his ear that splintered his bones and made blood flow from his mouth. Iros crashed to the ground, moaning and flailing, and he clenched his teeth, biting his tongue. I grabbed his feet and dragged him out while the Suitors, astonished but entertained, clapped and laughed. I left him at the entrance, put a stick in his hand, and gave him a few words.

"And now, act the palace guard and make sure no stray dogs or other animals get in."

Should I have rolled over and taken his insults and let that trash drive me from the palace? He said I ought to have stayed in the street, but this would not have served my and Telemachus' plans. The Suitors realized that I am not as weak as I appeared, but this will not make them fear that my presence could jeopardize their comfortable living. What's more, I have entertained them by flooring my rival, who perhaps was not a welcome presence even for them, with a single blow.

When the Suitors finally left for the palaestra at sunset, bringing with them some of the handmaidens with whom to vent their Dionysian lust under the gaze of the waning crescent moon, I was left alone with Telemachus and helped him remove all of the weapons from the hall, telling the handmaidens who were watching our moves that the smoke from the fireplace had blackened them and that it was time to polish them and protect them from the soot. Telemachus gave this explanation especially for Melantho, the worst of all the handmaidens, who was still masquerading herself before catching up with the others in the palaestra. A spy who without fail would tell the Suitors everything.

While I was carrying an armful of spears into the repository, Melantho came up to me, her breasts bared.

"Are you going to finally get out of this house, or are you planning on staying here forever along with your lice?"

Melantho is wicked to the core, but I didn't react to her provocation, and her poisonous voice only gave me new thirst for revenge.

At Telemachus' order, the fire in the great stone fireplace was rekindled from the still-glowing embers where pieces of meat had been roasted. Soon the flames were burning high from the cypress logs stacked on the bronze andirons, illuminating the great hall with a red light that danced along the walls in reflection.

The intoxicating smell of resin spread throughout the house from the crackling wood.

PENELOPE

Benevolent spirits have helped me so far, but the trick of the shroud, woven by day and undone at night, has been discovered by Melantho, who must certainly have told Antinous about it already. He has, in fact, increased his arrogance twofold in recent days, and there must be a reason for such behavior. It is said that Melantho spends many nights in bed with Antinous, and that the bed is her place for secrets. And they think I should accept the courtship of this epitome of lust?

I confronted Melantho, who had come into my rooms already masked and half-naked, perhaps to steal a bracelet or necklace as she has done more than once in the past.

"Watch yourself," I told her, "and try to put an end to your dirty intrigues. The gods do not wish your queen to become angry with you, for you would have a hard time of it if Odysseus should ever return to this palace. But even if he has fallen victim to the sea during his return voyage, Telemachus is a man now, and will know how to rightfully punish you. You knew that I wanted to speak with this vagabond and ask him about Odysseus, and you tried to run him off. Remember that human life is quite fragile and that a single stroke of the sword could make your mischievous head roll in the dust. Keep in mind that Antinous' protection will not be enough to save you."

The worst of my handmaidens, aghast, lowered her head and walked off in silence at my words.

I have gotten dressed and perfumed and placed a light-red Egyptian linen poppy in my hair, purchased from a traveling merchant on our island, so as to greet this old vagabond with full honor, as if he were a prince. And in truth, it seems that his origins are indeed princely, as Telemachus says, even if bad luck has turned him into a vagabond and beggar. I don't know who to believe. There are so many, even among the Suitors, who claim noble origins but who are really descendants of coarse woodcutters like Ctesippus or from a family of cowherds like Amphinomus.

As much as my melancholy weighs upon me, I am still the queen of Ithaca and must maintain the decorum that my rank imposes for all occasions, especially before a foreigner. When he leaves this island and heads back into the world, I wouldn't want him to say that the queen of Ithaca does not show herself before guests with the dignified appearance that the solemn duty of hospitality demands.

ODYSSEUS

Penelope doesn't really have that languishing, withered look that I expected. From what Eumaios and even Telemachus told me, I was certain that I would find her eyes as beautiful as ever but consumed by tears, and the signs of lengthy agony on her lovely face. I admit that I would have preferred to see her looking less beautiful and radiant, as if in confirmation of how my long absence has weighed on her, leaving lines about her lips or crow's feet about her eyes, or some tremor or uncertainty in her voice. But there's none of this. It is truly strange how my position makes me wish that the woman I love with all my strength were less beautiful.

Penelope entered the great hall with a large red flower in her hair and a light white linen tunic which hinted at the perfect shape of her still-young body beneath it. Her face is more beautiful than I remembered it. I was struck by the sharp lines of her profile, of her polished face, like a marble bust. A discovery and a thrill. Men never know their women's profiles, they never look at them from the side. They may know every detail from the front, the color and the sparkle of their eyes, the shape of their lips, the hue of their cheeks, the line of their foreheads, but they almost always ignore their profiles.

Now I understand why the Suitors set up camp in my palace. They are here to struggle over my kingdom's riches and my royal title, yes, but also for the favor of a beautiful and enchanting woman. And that red linen flower that Penelope has placed in her hair—who gave it to her? Antinous perhaps, or one of her other admirers? I should be happy to find such a self-confident, such a changed Penelope. Instead, it makes me suffer, and I'm tormented by a thousand jealous thoughts.

Penelope had me take a seat on a stool in front of her own chair, which had been moved in front of the fireplace for the occasion. She did not immediately begin asking me questions about Odysseus, as I had expected, but rather wanted to hear my own story, from whence I arrived, where I was born, and which voyages I had undertaken before landing in this itinerant and desperate condition on the coast of Ithaca. I repeated my tale of a childhood in Crete, of palace life surrounded by servants, of my adventures at sea, of the long years camped under the walls of Troy—never once mentioning the name of Odysseus—of travels in Egypt and of my misadventures caused by my companions' misdeeds, and finally of my return trip aboard a Phoenician pirate ship and my escape from them while they were moored along the coast of Ithaca.

Penelope listened to my long story without once thinking that it was Odysseus himself before her.

In conclusion to my tale, I humbly said to Penelope, "My queen, I admire your beauty and elegance, your valor, and the strength of character that keeps you alive."

Penelope held up her hand to stop my compliments, which were required as a token of gratitude for the honor that she had bestowed upon me, and said that since Odysseus had left for Troy with the Achaeans, everything had changed on the island of Ithaca, whose fame and prosperity would be much different today if she had not been left alone to confront the Suitors who have invaded and pillaged her home.

Penelope interrupted my story from time to time to ask for more details about my adventures, even inquiring what foods the Phoenician pirates gave me to eat and whether or not I had had amorous adventures during my travels. A truly strange question, to which I replied that there were two prostitutes on board the pirate ship to satisfy the needs of the sailors but not of the prisoners, and that at every stop along the coast the pirates went on the prowl for young women, who were then raped and abandoned before the locals were able to react. I said, my voice breaking, that when I departed Crete on my adventures, I had left behind my infant son and a woman who loved me, and whom I had never seen since, and that after twenty years I dared not present myself to her in my current condition, an old man reduced to begging.

Seated on the stool in front of Penelope, who listened attentively to my words, I spun my lying tales with verve and authenticity, controlling my emotions in order to avoid the tears that have so often cascaded down my face like a swollen river ever since I arrived in Ithaca.

I watched Penelope in the reddish light of the fire, her every glance distracting my train of thought, and the only way for me to escape her seductive power was by lowering my eyes and diving into my imaginary past. Finally Penelope told me that she had been waiting for many years to have news about Odysseus, but that she had received nothing more than vague and often lying rumors. And so if I had reliable news, no matter how small or fragmentary, would I please speak, choosing my words carefully so as not to give her any vain hopes.

"Then I will tell you, gentle queen, that the first time I saw the intrepid Odysseus was beneath the walls of Troy, and that I saw him once again after the war near the coast of Trinacria where the tempestuous winds had blown him off course, pushing his ship between the two sea monsters of Scylla and Charybdis. It was during that encounter that he told me of his voyage to Crete, where he was treated graciously within the walls of my own palace, which had fallen into the hands of usurpers. They were generous, however, offering him the treatment worthy of a king and showing the proper hospitality to all of his companions. When he described every detail of the palace that was no longer mine and told me of my wife and grown son, now reduced to poverty and awaiting my arrival in a house outside of the city, I wept. I had to tell him to stop, so much pain did his every word cause me. When the impetuous Boreas was once again bottled up by Aeolus and the sea became calm, Odysseus sailed away from the island of Trinacria, he himself gripping the helm, the ship pointed straight toward Ithaca. But I've heard that he was shipwrecked, and that he saved himself by swimming to the island of the Phaeacians."

Her face remained motionless, and her expression as still as a statue, yet tears streamed down Penelope's cheeks as she listened to the seafaring tragedies of Odysseus. But she steadied herself and asked whether I could prove that I was telling the truth. Could I, for example, tell her what clothes Odysseus was wearing in those long-ago days when he arrived in Troy? What else did I remember about him and his companions?

I deliberately paused before speaking, as if I was looking into the deep well of memory to find images left there twenty years earlier. I then began to speak slowly, as if the images and memories of the past were only vaguely coming to the surface.

"Odysseus wore a crimson mantle," I said, "and he kept it fastened beneath his chin by a gold clasp in the form of a dog that held a deer between its paws. I remember the clasp well, for it was admired by everyone, just as I remember the soft tunic that covered the warrior's body. But I cannot say whether the mantle and tunic were the clothes he was wearing when he left Ithaca or if they were gifts from his hosts during the many stops made on the long voyage to Troy. He must have received many gifts during his travels because—I hope you will not be displeased, gentle queen—Odysseus was well loved by all, especially women, who always looked upon him with desire, their eyes sparkling. And I can also remember, now that my memories are becoming clearer, that he was always in the company of a dark-skinned herald with curly hair."

At these words, Penelope let forth a quickly stifled sob. She herself had woven that crimson mantle and placed it on her husband's shoulders, she said, just as she had pinned its two flaps with the golden clasp.

A kind handmaiden came swiftly to her queen's aid to comfort her with a cup of hot infusion sweetened with honey.

Penelope accepted it with thanks and wanted me to have a cup of that foul drink as well, as a reward for my stories. But after this initial show of emotion, Penelope asked no more questions, as if her interest in Odysseus, her much-beloved Odysseus as she said, had suddenly vanished. Resignation? Indifference? The tedium of memories? Oh, how the years sprinkle a choking dust on our emotions. Has Ithaca lost its memory?

I wanted to continue with my story in order to test Penelope's interest in her husband. I told of how during the siege of Troy I had seen Odysseus walking the beach one evening holding a large, shiny pink shell to his ear.

"'It is said that you can hear all the noises of the sea inside a shell,' I said to Odysseus, 'the crashing waves, the whistling wind, the howling tempests, the shrieking of gulls. But here we are at the sea's edge, so why listen to it in a shell?'"

"'I don't listen to the sea in this shell,' Odysseus replied. 'I listen to the voice of my wife, the voice of my beloved Penelope, who speaks to me from far-off Ithaca. I close my eyes and hear her voice, and that of my baby boy Telemachus, who is crying and stammering out his first words.'"

"It made me weep, sweet queen, and I was again full of admiration for Odysseus, who always knew how to use his cleverness to make up for the worst of circumstances. And I have heard that even after a terrible shipwreck he came ashore with his talking shell, and that he often holds it to his ear to comfort himself in moments of melancholy."

"This is the first time," Penelope said, "that I have heard anyone suggest that Odysseus can be melancholy. It surprises me, but it is true that men are not made of stone, and that even they can change with time and circumstance. This tale of the seashell, so touching in itself, is completely new to me, just as the image of a melancholic Odysseus is a novelty. But emotions are sometimes more fleeting than the men who feel them."

Penelope did not wish to make any further comments, but her voice, at least to me, seemed to be swallowed down all at once, snuffed out at the bottom of her throat. She turned and watched the flame that flickered above the spitting wood in the fireplace. Did she want to hide another outburst of emotion? More tears?

PENELOPE

Ordeals of a voyage after a bloody war, struggles against a cruel sea, an adventuresome spirit buffeted by winds and salt air, lonely nights under a hostile sky, a homeland turned upside down by greedy, wicked lords vying for his wife's hand—can any of these misfortunes atone for the mistrust and suspicion that stoke this man's heart against his beloved?

If the feeling we call love remained alive in his heart during these years of separation, if Odysseus truly convinced himself that he could hear my voice inside a shell, then why transform this love into suffering, why poison it with suspicion? When I heard this vagabond's voice for the first time, and locked eyes with him for a single instant, I knew.

In spite of his ragged clothes, the artfully bent spine, the trembling hands that feigned old age, regardless of how his fingernails wandered from time to time underneath those rags and into his greasy, mud-caked hair to make us believe that fleas and lice were dwelling there, I knew instantly that the man sitting on that stool near the burning fire in front of my eyes was my husband, the man I have longed for during twenty years of sleepless nights and anxious days passed in my palace, assaulted by rowdy Suitors.

And so after ten years spent sailing from one end of the earth to the other on a voyage that should have lasted no longer than a single year, Odysseus is home, and mistrusts his wife to such an extent that he prefers to reveal his identity to Telemachus— who in fact has welcomed him in like a friend—rather than confide himself in the woman who has suffered so much over his absence. And Telemachus is already behaving like the man his father Odysseus teaches him to be, no longer trusting even his own mother with his secrets.

How can I rejoice over Odysseus' return if he persists in coming before me in the clothes of an aged beggar, if I cannot stroke his long, unkempt beard and his sunburnt, windswept face, if I cannot even embrace him as I desire? I sometimes awake in the morning with tears in my eyes because the world is falling to pieces around me and I am suffocating under the rubble. Why doesn't Odysseus come to my rescue? Why does he hide himself from his wife?

Fine. If that's how he wants it, so be it. I can play this game of fictions too, and we'll see who knows how to dissemble best.

ODYSSEUS

Penelope didn't recognize me. She called for the handmaidens and ordered them to bring decent clothes for me to wear, and she promised that I would partake in regular meals inside the palace walls as recompense for my stories, and then asked if I would give her permission to have my flea-ridden rags burned.

"Of course, my queen," I answered, "but not today. And I would like to save my satchel forever as a reminder of my long voyages over land and sea, the same satchel that I filled with food for my survival. You can't imagine how attached a vagabond can grow to an item of clothing or an object like this one. When you don't have a house, when you live the solitary life of a wanderer, you end up turning an insignificant possession into your travel companion, like a precious talisman, even if it is mud-caked and greasy."

And so Penelope ordered the handmaidens to wash my greasy satchel with hot ashes.

What I can't understand is why Penelope takes every chance she gets to speak of other things. She never asked me when I saw Odysseus for the last time, whether he was in good health, how he was feeling, or what words he spoke. Nothing. It is terribly strange how her curiosity about Odysseus seemed to dry up the moment she understood that I was speaking the truth. She almost seems more interested in listening to tales about the long-ago siege of Troy, tales that she has certainly heard a thousand times from a thousand speakers, rather than news about his return.

Is Penelope's love stuck in that distant past? Is that why she sobbed when I told her about the crimson mantle and golden clasp? Is she perhaps afraid of hearing unflattering news about Odysseus in more recent days? I don't want to think, even for a second, that her love has faded with the years, or under the attentions of these young admirers. But what do I know about her life during this endless period of twenty years?

She never fails to show her annoyance over the Suitors who have set up camp in her palace: to Telemachus, to her most faithful handmaidens, even to the swineherd Eumaios. But really, which woman on earth wouldn't be flattered by so many young, royal admirers circling around her? Might it only be the herds of animals being slaughtered day after day that upsets her?

"Sweet queen," I said, "do you still think about those far-off days when Odysseus left for the Trojan War, a war that you have rightly called useless? Maybe your feelings are trapped in those unhappy days and you no longer care much to know whether Odysseus is still among the living or if he has fallen amongst the shades of Hades. If that is the case, I will no longer tell pointless stories that intrude upon your desire for peace, and perhaps a new marriage."

I expected these goading words to cause Penelope to take offense and proclaim her undying love for Odysseus, which Telemachus and even the swineherd Eumaios have inclined me to believe in. Instead, only more tears that spilled over for events far in the past, tears of resignation and of regret for a happiness that she has lost and can never recover.

Penelope stared at the flames in the fireplace, and in a voice barely above a whisper, as if she were ashamed of herself, finally asked me if I thought that Odysseus was still among the living and, if so, whether I knew anything about the most recent progress of his travels. So I twisted the truth in order to root out her real feelings. I said once again that I knew for certain that after losing all of his companions to the sea, Odysseus had landed naked and alone on the island of the Phaeacians, where he was welcomed with royal honors and showered with precious gifts.

"From the island of the Phaeacians," I said, "Odysseus should already be sailing toward Ithaca. I truly thought I would find him here, but perhaps the sailing is slower than expected, either because of the sea or because of his restless and curious nature, causing him to stop in every harbor that he spies, wanting to meet new people and accumulate more treasure. Or maybe he has lost faith in his wife's feelings and is afraid that he will not be welcomed in Ithaca as he hopes. How can the good Odysseus know whether Penelope has been constant, or if she has given her favors to one of her admirers?"

Penelope did not show the joy that I wanted to see upon hearing this news of Odysseus' imminent arrival. She simply said that she had never lost hope, and then she called her handmaidens and ordered them to wash my feet as if I were a high-born guest.

"This way you can be seated at our table next to Telemachus, and you will be respected by all the lords and served by the handmaidens and servants. And other maids will prepare a bed for you tonight with a soft wool blanket."

Then she added that perhaps the angry gods would never allow her to see Odysseus again, as they had already put so many obstacles in his path during his voyage. But if it was Odysseus himself who had given in to his desire for adventure, then the trip from the island of the Phaeacians to Ithaca might last another ten years.

What on earth has Telemachus been thinking? Where is the despairing Penelope, whose face is consumed by tears and who spends sleepless nights counting the stars in the sky? And the good and honest Eumaios—what fables has he been spinning under the roof of his hut? It seems as though Penelope doesn't hope at all for Odysseus' return. Maybe his arrival would ruin her plans for a new marriage with one of the Suitors? Antinous is clearly the chosen one; haughty, powerful, proud Antinous, who already moves about my palace like a king, giving orders to the handmaidens, and who lords over the other pretenders. How bitter the truth can be, and how different from Telemachus' naive dreams and imagination.

"No impure woman shall touch your feet," Penelope told me. "You will be washed by the old nurse of Odysseus himself, your companion, which is the greatest honor I can give to you."

"I want nothing more, my beloved queen," I replied, "than to be touched by the same hands that once cared for the man whom

I admire more than any other, and who will one day arrive in his homeland not dressed as a beggar like my unfortunate self, but triumphantly, laden with precious gifts from the Phaeacians and from the other cities that he visited during his journey home."

At a sign from Penelope, old Eurycleia came toward me carrying a silver basin, mixing cold water with boiling water taken from the fire, saying that she would be most honored to wash the feet of a man who was the friend of her king, whom she had held in her arms and cared for since birth. The old nurse looked into my eyes and suddenly told me that she had never before met anyone who looked so similar to her lord Odysseus.

It was almost like Eurycleia wanted to sniff me, the way dogs do to recognize someone, just as my dog Argos had done, and then she touched me to confirm what her eyes, tired in their old age but still very wise, were telling her. So I said that many people before had told me of this resemblance between myself and Odysseus, though my travails and the hand of a hostile god now made me look older than my actual years.

When old Eurycleia's hands, holding a sponge, moved up my leg to my calf, they found the thick scar that the tusk of a fierce wild boar had left on me when, as a young man, I had gone hunting on Mount Helicon with my noble grandfather Autolycos. The wild beast had burst from the thick underbrush and wounded me with its tusk before I struck it down with my spear. The wound healed, but it left a permanent scar, and when the old woman touched it with her trembling hand, she looked deep into my eyes, about to say something and dash all of my plans for secrecy.

I clamped a hand over my old nurse's mouth and gave her a sign to keep quiet. Eurycleia was momentarily confused, then she understood that my situation required her silence, and she wisely held her breath, swallowing down the words of joy that would have come from her mouth like the tears brimming in her eyes.

Eurycleia had let my foot slip from her hands and splash water from the basin all over the floor, and though Penelope saw this, she suspected nothing more than that the old nurse's hands were weak—not that I had been recognized—since Eurycleia quickly got up for more water and for the olive oil that she would use to massage my legs.

I stood up to help her, and whispered in a voice that Penelope could not hear that no one could know Odysseus had returned, or it would be the ruin of myself and my house. Not a single word, then, not even to Penelope. Eurycleia quietly replied that despite her age, her heart was as solid as a rock and her will as strong as iron. She seemed pleased to share such an important secret with her king.

When Eurycleia had finished the washing and anointed my feet and calves with olive oil, we all ate a light meal in silence. At the end of the meal, Penelope declared that it was time for her to retire, and she asked the old nurse to show me to the room where a bed had been prepared. I followed Eurycleia's faltering steps across the hall at my own slow pace, pretending to aid myself with my cane. I told myself that I could trust her more than my Penelope, so withdrawn and troubled by dark thoughts.

While she showed me my bed and before wishing me sweet dreams, Eurycleia tried to reassure me, repeating that her heart was as solid as a rock and her will as strong as iron. She waited for me to lie down on a large ox skin, then she covered my shoulders with a soft sheepskin and large wool blanket. She left after wishing me a good night.

As I lay there, sailing the waves of a thousand thoughts that kept me from sleep, disturbed by the words spoken by Penelope, so distant, so seemingly resigned, maybe determined to give herself over to the noblest of her admirers, I heard a great scampering going on behind the columns as handmaidens went to lie with the youngest of the Suitors, just returning from the palaestra.

I heard their purring voices, their lewd laughter echoing in the dark, their amorous moans from improvised beds behind the columns and in the corners of the great hall. An implacable anger clutched at my chest and I wanted nothing else than to take up a sword and spill the blood of those profaning my home, but I had to hold myself back from my thirst for revenge, awaiting the right moment to kill them off one by one like beasts in a slaughterhouse. Only a massacre can wash away this outrage and free Ithaca from these usurpers.

Endure this torment too, I told myself, just as you endured the hostility of the gods who fed your companions to the devouring Cyclops and drowned them under the waves of the sea.

PENELOPE

I need to shield myself from the memories that have guided my every move and thought for years. The lightest of movements, almost floating on air, and the heaviest of thoughts, like lead. When I recognized Odysseus under those vagrant's rags, I realized to my infinite sadness that he places no trust in me—the woman who shared years of youth and joy, who once spoke soft words and made love to him. Our best years have withered away in memories, and Odysseus has lost the mysterious promise of real passions, of the desires that every woman in the world is entitled to, his wife included.

Odysseus fought the Sirens, the Cyclopes, and the Sea Monsters that he found in his path and is now suspicious of everyone everywhere, believing himself to be in a state of perpetual war with the world. And thus his return is joyless, and comes under a cloud of suspicion. How can I forgive Odysseus for this mask of coldness behind which he studies me like an inanimate object?

When the old nurse was washing his legs with her sponge, I hid my face in the shadows, but I was watching her every move in order to see how Odysseus would react at the moment when she inevitably recognized him. I saw Eurycleia's body jerk, and I watched Odysseus cover her mouth with his hand so she would not speak, then stand up and help her fetch more water for the basin despite the fact that he was barefoot.

How naive the cunning Odysseus is. And how naive he assumes the rest of us to be. While Troy was under siege, his cunning proved victorious more than once, and even during his return voyage it seems that he was able to escape from the Cyclopes, the Sea Monsters, and a thousand other obstacles through trickery. But just as he is able to slip from every real difficulty, so with equal stubbornness does Odysseus go looking for obstacles everywhere, and when he does not find them, he invents them himself, as if he wanted to test his own craft and intelligence time and time again. But I am not an enemy scheming against him, nor a cheating wife. If he won't trust me, I will feed his mistrust; if he injures me with new venom, I will repay him with the same.

I've already thrown his ham-handed comedy into disarray by showing indifference to the story of Odysseus' return to Ithaca. It was an easy game to play, because I had Odysseus there before my very eyes, seated next to the fireplace, and therefore had nothing more to fear from a perilous sea or other dangers plotted by the gods. Odysseus was there, with his ragged cloak on his back, acting out his play while he leaned on a cane like an old man. His simplistic disguise would have made me burst out laughing had my dark thoughts allowed it, had I not feared the swords and daggers of the Suitors lying in wait here in his house.

Telemachus' return has made the Suitors nervous, and soon their tensions will run wild like a forest fire. But they don't know—wretched men—that Odysseus is already among them. His disguise didn't fool me, and not even Eurycleia was taken in by it, but the Suitors are dull, haughty men and they neither realize nor even suspect who is hidden beneath those beggar's rags.

Odysseus' refusal to take me into his confidence and make use of my help is the cause of a bitterness as boundless as the sky. Yet I cannot unburden myself to anyone, because even the old, faithful Eurycleia has been bewitched by Odysseus and keeps her lips sealed. I speak to myself like those who have lost their senses, or like a drunk woman—me, who never touches wine.

Like a good sailor who sounds the rocky coast while he is sailing, Odysseus is testing the waters, but he will have a hard time probing the secrets of my soul, for I too know how to pretend as needed; I've had long years of practice doing so to protect myself from the assault of the Suitors, from their flattery, from their servants' intrigues. More than once have I had to throw asphodel flowers, stinking of death, from my bedroom window, where enemy handmaidens had left them for me.

Poor Odysseus, how I hate him, and how I love him despite everything, even dressed in those sickening beggar's rags.

ODYSSEUS

Penelope asked Telemachus why he had removed all of the weapons from the palace hall and where he had hidden them. Telemachus explained to his mother that the constantly burning fire had made the shiny blades smoky, and that this was the reason for hiding the weapons until he could get a blacksmith to polish them. But those weapons, Penelope explained, belong to the Suitors, and before removing them from the hall he should have asked their permission. And that it would have been sufficient to order the handmaidens to polish them the same way they polish the copper pots. Did not this impudence risk raising the anger of the Suitors?

"Anger without weapons will not cause much damage," Telemachus replied, "but since my return, the presence of those swords and spears could spark fatal duels in the house where we live."

"Would you be so upset if the Suitors killed one another off?" Penelope asked.

"And if your son was among the victims of these duels, as they seem to be planning?" Telemachus said.

Penelope made no further comment.

I praised Telemachus for not revealing to his mother the real reason for hiding the Suitors' weapons, but I think she has sensed that something dangerous is going to happen soon in the palace. Penelope has a quick and penetrating mind, but the presence of Telemachus and the news of an impending arrival by Odysseus, as much as she pretends not to believe it, have convinced her to be prudent and keep silent. I don't want to cast doubt on Penelope's faithfulness, but a few of her statements about Antinous have made me think that she is finally resigned to accepting his marriage proposal. And I am afraid that she is soon to suggest this solution to Telemachus as a way toward peace. Or is this just my imagination and jealousy?

Telemachus, who swears on his mother's faithfulness, fears that her exhaustion has worn down her spirit as much as her physical strength, and that she is near collapse. I don't get that feeling—Penelope looks as solid as a rock—but I still think it necessary for her not to discover my identity. In spite of her ambiguities, I am sure that when the moment comes, she will take our side, and this is enough for me. What am I saying? This is not enough for me.

The disappearance of the weapons from the great palace hall must have unnerved Penelope, who chose to tell me about a dream as if I were one of those fortune-tellers who give wild interpretations to images from the night.

"Twenty white geese," she told me, "were eating grains of wheat here in the house and I was watching them with pleasure. I love all birds, and I consider geese to be birds of good fortune and peace because of their pure white feathers. But all of a sudden a brilliant eagle flew inside flapping its wings and with its hooked beak broke the necks of each of those peaceful birds, who were left bloody on the floor. After the slaughter, the eagle came to me as I was crying and said the following words: Do not despair over this slaughter, for you must know that the geese who peck the wheat in your house are none other than your admirers. The avenging eagle is none other than Odysseus, who has returned to his home after many vicissitudes to bring death to the Suitors. After these words in a human voice, the eagle spread its wings and flew around the interior of the great hall twice before finally flying out of the window and disappearing in the black sky."

"I think," I said to Penelope, "that the eagle has already given you an interpretation of this dream, in which you yourself are the protagonist. The only oddity is that in your dream, the Suitors are represented by birds of good fortune and peace. As for the rest of it, I don't know what I could add to the words of the great bird except that I have also heard that Odysseus is at sea and will soon land at Ithaca to take revenge for the violent occupation of his house and conjugal bed."

Penelope's body jerked at these words.

"How dare you, stranger, think that Odysseus' conjugal bed has been profaned by the presence of another man?"

"My sweet queen," I told Penelope, "I would never on my own have dared to think such infamous things. But last night, after I had lain down on the bed that you had prepared for my night's rest, I heard the handmaidens making love with the young Suitors in the corners of the great hall and behind the columns, and they were joking and gossiping among themselves. I heard one of these handmaidens whispering that Antinous, being your chosen one, often climbs to the upper rooms and spends the night in Odysseus' bed. This is what the handmaiden said and I merely repeat her words to you. I understand that the handmaiden's words may be unpleasant, but I thought it right to tell you the words I heard inside your house. If, though, you believe that I have been in error to repeat this infamy to you, I humbly ask your forgiveness and I promise that I will erase the sound of those words from my mind and cast them into the deep dark of oblivion forever."

PENELOPE

I can't decide whether these rumors attributed to the handmaidens were truly said or are simply an invention by Odysseus to test my feelings. I already knew that the handmaidens spend their nights making love with the Suitors, and it is certainly no surprise that their tongues are as poisonous as snakes, but I can't believe that Antinous boasts of having been in my bed. I think it would be an insult to his intelligence and pride. Unless, since there is a tacit understanding among the Suitors that he is the chosen one for marriage, he thinks that he can make a down payment on my body by spreading these rumors. The only certainty is that Odysseus' words betray, alas, his horrible suspicions.

More than one night have I left my bed and tiptoed to the stairs to listen to the moans of the handmaidens making love with the Suitors, and in those moments my senses were reawakened and an intense agitation disturbed my entire body, calling before my eyes the image of Odysseus with his words of love and his hard body, smooth as bronze. I didn't betray him even in my thoughts. But I never would have imagined that those vipers would accuse their queen of depraved couplings like those that occupy their own nights.

I confess that I envied those handmaidens who were able to satisfy their desires while I spent my nights wasting away in loneliness with only memories of my husband. But why on earth, if Odysseus' words are true, do they wish to associate me with their vices? Do they think that they will seem more regal by throwing mud on my character? Unfortunately, the ingratitude of servants is a menace seen throughout the history of the world.

ODYSSEUS

Penelope hints that Antinous is the primary candidate for taking my place in her bed, but it is unclear from her words whether he has been chosen by the Suitors or by herself. It looks as if she truly doesn't believe in my imminent return, but she promised me gifts and hospitality when I said it was so.

It seems as if she has come to accept the presence of the Suitors as an inescapable situation, but she complains about their eating all her provisions and herds. So it's no more than a problem of sheep, oxen, and wine? I don't think she is making plans for a future with Odysseus, and maybe she thinks that even if I were to return I would not have the strength to defeat these ranks of warlike and violent young men who are so intent on maintaining their privileges. Help me, O gods of Olympus, to understand my wife. Why are you laughing? What is there to laugh about?

Why was Penelope so concerned when she discovered that Telemachus had hidden the Suitors' weapons? What kind of secrets and how much confusion are hidden in her soul? By now, I no longer know whether the dream about the geese and the eagle expresses a fear or a desire. I'm sailing blindly in unknown waters and the winds buffet me in one direction and then another and make my relationship with Penelope more and more difficult. Her every word, her every movement leaves an ambiguous mark on my memory. I have defended myself from water and fire, from iron and other metals, from stones, from the earth, from illness, from four-legged creatures and one-eyed monsters, from birds, from the Sirens, and from the jealousy of the gods, but I don't know how to defend myself from Penelope.

Poor Odysseus. Without ever losing hope you got yourself out of even the toughest dangers of the war and you avoided the infinite traps that the gods laid in your path, and now you watch your wife as if she were an ineffable ghost even though she is seated there in front of you and all you need to do is reach out your hand to touch her.

Telemachus would like to take me to see my elderly father Laertes in his house outside the city. What a naive idea. Visiting my elderly father would reveal my identity to everyone and sound the alarm for the Suitors, just now when lightning bolts are flashing through all of the rooms of the palace, heralding a storm. The handmaidens are fighting amongst themselves and screeching over nothing, like animals who have sensed a coming danger. A cook knifed an errand boy during an argument and an army of ants has invaded the chest where the honey is kept. And they say a serpent entered the kitchen and another was found hanging from the engorged teats of a cow. I have waited many years to see my elderly father, and I can wait a few more days.

Won't the Suitors be worried, after seeing me knock the arrogant Iros down with a single, well-balanced blow, that they have a dangerous energumen in their midst? Even more so since I was invited into the palace by Telemachus, who has insisted upon my presence in spite of their taunts, and who has poured my wine with his own hands as if I were an honored guest. Every time I see them speaking together I prick up my ears to hear if I am the subject of their conversation, but I have discovered nothing that casts light on their thoughts. Perhaps the only thoughts that occupy the dim-witted minds of the Suitors are roasting the meat that the herdsmen bring daily, drinking the wine from my grottoes, and making love to the handmaidens at night. And waiting for Penelope to surrender.

I'm so accustomed to living under the open sky, exposed to all the winds, that after a while inside the house I feel like I am suffocating, and I need to get out to breathe the streaming air, to move my arms and legs. When I passed the doorway and found Iros nearby, resigned by now to playing the guardian and keeping stray dogs from entering the palace, the beggar looked at me with curiosity.

"Who are you really? Where do you come from? And what are you hiding?"

"Don't worry your head about it," I replied, but his questions gave me reason for concern.

I have learned from experience, an experience that I admit is limited to the rags I am wearing, that beggars, even the most stupid and arrogant like Iros, have a finely honed eye and always notice things above and beyond appearances. I would not want to have him recognize me and sound the alarm with the Suitors.

I have adapted my actions to the rags that I wear, and so I spit on his feet and immediately returned inside without even looking him in the face.

Not until late morning did Penelope appear in the great hall, her shoulders covered by a woolen mantle embroidered with golden thread and a lapis lazuli necklace around her neck. Who knows if this mantle and this necklace are gifts from the Suitors. She certainly didn't have them when I left for the Trojan War.

For the moment, I simply expressed my admiration for the noble aspect of her clothes and the beauty of the lapis lazuli necklace that sparkled from the golden specks inside the intense blue of the stones. Penelope thanked me with a smile, but when I asked her if Ithaca by any chance had lapis lazuli quarries, she deliberately kept from telling me where the necklace came from. In so doing, she confirmed my suspicion that she had received it as a gift from one of the Suitors. It must be him, Antinous.

Penelope plays the part of the queen. Fine. She is indeed the queen, but I don't recall her being so hard and restrained, so inflexible. She began by saying a few inconsequential words about the drought that is ruining the crops and has dried out the pastures.

"Drought and a strong sun make good, strong wine," I said.

"I'm glad for the winemakers," she replied, "even though I don't like wine."

She said she was worried about the rutted roads, about the undersized bakery, and she spoke to me about the need to dig a new cistern in order to increase water reserves. The palaestra is abandoned and only Dionysian orgies are held there. Thus

Penelope takes an interest in agriculture and the problems of the city. Maybe she wanted to have me understand that she is taking care of her subjects so I will speak about it when I return to my wandering of the world, as she believes I will do.

Then she returned once again to her rooms and called for Telemachus, whom she stayed with for quite a while.

This is the first time since I have arrived that I observed Penelope up close by the light of day. She is extraordinarily beautiful; she has preserved all of her freshness, her long black hair, her sea-blue eyes. She seemed such a fragile woman those many years ago when I left Ithaca, and I thought that she would have suffered greatly over my absence, but now I find her fortified in her soul, self-assured, and actively governing the island. I spoke about her many times with my companions, but I was speaking about another woman. I left behind a soft, attentive young wife, and I have discovered a hard woman, full of mysteries, perhaps even more seductive than before, but different, very different.

I wonder. That lapis lazuli necklace and that golden mantle that I don't recognize, where do they come from? All these years, Penelope won't have always been sitting by the window listening to birdsong or watching the pageant of the sunset. She has changed so much. For the better? For the worse? Occasionally I forget that I am Odysseus and I myself feel like a stranger in this house, near this woman. And this constant thought about Antinous won't leave me alone. He is younger than me, maybe even than her. He is strong and daring.

I wish Penelope had recognized me, in spite of the danger. I secretly hoped so, but nothing came of it, and she treats me with the slightly detached politeness that one can concede to a poor vagabond and shows me small gestures of kindness that you usually show to the elderly. Is it the disguise that has tricked her, or have I really aged so much? And why doesn't she ever look me in the eye? I'm certain that Eurycleia recognized me even before touching my scar with her hands, but for Penelope I am just a poor wanderer who deserves a bit of attention because he was Odysseus' companion under the walls of Troy. It all saddens me to tears, goddamn tears.

I decided not to accept any clothes that they offered me and insisted on keeping the miserable articles that I arrived in, in order to hide my identity from the Suitors. From Penelope too, out of extreme caution. I've been all too successful.

I arrived in Ithaca with the lacerating idea of reconquering my land and testing Penelope's faithfulness, and I find myself as lost and confused as the vagabond that I am pretending to be, someone with no skills for thought. I have to admit that it is easier to predict the moves of your enemy in war than the thoughts of naive Penelope. A clever vixen.

The handmaidens carried a platter of roasted meat and a pitcher of wine upstairs. I will ask Telemachus if Penelope herself is drinking the wine. She didn't drink it when I left and she just told me that she doesn't like it. Everything astonishes me, and everything makes me suspicious.

Telemachus came downstairs before sunrise and told me that Penelope has made a decision that left me slack-jawed. She told him that she would like to hold a competition among the Suitors, a game that I used to offer once a year to all of the princes of the island and nearby lands. Twelve axes would be set upright in a perfectly straight line in the great hall, and the challenge was to shoot an arrow from my own bow through the twelve rings of the axes. But that was not the hard part. For many years, I alone was able to string my powerful bow and send the arrow through the twelve rings.

Now Penelope is offering herself as a prize. She has decided that she will marry the Suitor who wins the competition.

I was shocked by Penelope's idea. First of all because it means that she has decided to put an end to the Suitors' wait. Penelope knows perfectly well that for many years this competition was won by Odysseus and that no one was ever able to string his bow, but she also knows that the only possible victor is Antinous, the chief and most powerful among her admirers. Or perhaps she hopes that no one will win the competition and that the wedding will be delayed longer?

The announcement of the competition coincides with the decision Telemachus and I made to hide the Suitors' weapons. This could mean that Penelope wants to take advantage of this disarmament because she knows that mortal conflict among the Suitors could be an outcome of this competition. Or has she, I wonder, somehow found out from the old nurse that Odysseus is here in the palace and hopes that he will take part in the competition? No, I cannot believe that Eurycleia didn't keep the promise she made to her king.

It is equally clear that the dream about the geese and the eagle has foreseen the massacre of the Suitors that I have planned with Telemachus. A desire? A fantasy? A coincidence? Unless the dream was simply made up by Penelope to express her hopes. Has she told it to the Suitors as well? Suddenly, everything seems to have gone mad, and the mischievous Dionysus seems to have taken over the island.

How fast thoughts fly in the dark, how they run. After a night's sleep more agitated than the sea between Scylla and Charybdis, I awoke with swollen eyes and a bitter taste in my mouth. I took my ox hide outdoors and carefully arranged the sheepskins and wool mantle from my bed on a stool. I assured

Telemachus that old Eurycleia had provided me with a pleasant night's sleep. Why worry him with stories about my nocturnal anxieties?

In front of the palace, meanwhile, the servant boys were chopping wood while the handmaidens rekindled the fire in the large fireplace and other handmaidens swept the floor of the scattered remains from the previous day. And while they cleaned the great hall, they muttered curses at the Suitors for their lack of consideration toward the house and for not behaving like guests, but rather like insolent and dissipated masters.

Even the repugnant Melanthius arrived early from the countryside, tying four young goats for the Suitors' banquet under the portico. The goatherd didn't waste the chance to complain once again about my presence.

"If you keep begging in this house," he said maliciously, "sooner or later we will come to blows, and I will drive you away by force from this place that wishes to see your face no more."

I would have liked to tell him to go take a bath in the sea since he stank nauseatingly of goat, but I held back the rage that inflamed my heart and once again did not respond to his reproaches, as prudence recommended. And meanwhile, there outside, near the entrance, the shiftless Iros had started singing obscene songs in his animal voice.

Then good Philoetius, the oxherd, also came to the palace, bringing a cow to slaughter, and he passed the time with the swineherd Eumaios by counting the animals devoured by the Suitors. They would have gladly rebelled against this waste, but they knew that their only way to avoid punishment was by keeping their mouths shut, because the goatherd Melanthius reported their every word. Melanthius detested them because he was afraid they would interfere in his collecting the horns of the slaughtered animals, which he then sold for a profit to Phoenician merchants. Once already, Ctesippus, spurred on by Melanthius, had tied Eumaios and Philoetius together by the hands and left them hanging from an old olive tree in the sun for an entire day. He answered anyone who asked him why he had done it by saying that he just wanted to have some fun, but the two herdsmen were sure that Melanthius had instigated his actions.

"I would have moved to another kingdom with all of my belongings a long time ago," Philoetius said, "where I could continue raising cattle, but I ultimately decided to wait for Odysseus' return to Ithaca. I simply can't miss the sight of our king skewering one after another of this mob of rascally usurpers like pieces of roasted meat on a spit. I want to see their blood flow like the cattle they butcher for their banquets."

Strange words, from which I confirmed that Ithaca is full of rumors of my imminent return. Eumaios, rabid with hate for the Suitors, would prefer to hang them all from their feet and give them a slow death so they would have reason to regret their foul deeds.

Meanwhile Amphinomus, the most voracious of all the Suitors, ordered the servile good-for-nothing Melanthius to cut the throats of the goats and the animals brought by the herdsmen in preparation for another banquet. The fire crackled in the fireplace and soon the spits, sizzling with fat, were being turned by two handmaidens, and as the pieces were roasted, the pantry maids placed the meat in baskets to bring to the table where the Suitors had already taken their places. Other handmaidens poured wine into large silver goblets and flitted about between them, showing off their bodies shamelessly.

Finally Telemachus brought food to me with his own hands, placing it on a stool close to the stone doorway where I had sat down, and he poured me some wine in a golden chalice.

"And now," he said loud enough for the Suitors to hear it, "you will come and sit among the princes, who will not dare to hurl insults upon you anymore, because you are my guest in my palace, just as they too are my guests."

As soon as I sat at the table next to Telemachus, here was Antinous who wished to speak to everyone with his usual haughtiness.

"Telemachus speaks loudly in order to scare us, but we, among all our possible reactions, can even choose to feel pity for his inexperience. But we ask him to thank us and father Zeus for having given him the gift of life."

"I am already aware of your many claims," Telemachus replied, "but until today I hadn't heard that your power was similar to that of father Zeus. Probably all the cattle and goats that you sacrifice every day for the pleasure of your divine nostrils and your bottomless bellies have gone to your heads."

After pronouncing these words, Telemachus took my arm, squeezing it tightly with his hand in order to keep me calm, while the pantry boy cut the meat and the handmaidens served it to everyone at the table.

Following Antinous, Ctesippus, the richest among all the admirers, the fat and pompous rival to Antinous and a man experienced in all forms of depravity, stood up to speak, his mouth full of food.

"I want to tell you all something, you hard-hearted admirers. Telemachus' guest has already had his portion of food, as is right for a scruffy old vagabond, but I too would like to give him a gift as a show of my generosity."

Having spoken thus, Ctesippus deftly grabbed a cow's hoof from the large basket on the table and threw it at me with unexpected violence.

I dodged the blow by lowering my head, and the hoof bounced off the wall and fell to the ground.

"You are very lucky that you didn't hit my guest," Telemachus then said, standing up; "otherwise I would have taken this spear and run it through your liver, and instead of the wedding you hope for, you would have gotten a deep tomb, maybe even decorated with precious marble since you are so rich, but you would never have eaten the animals from my herds, nor drunk the wine from my grottoes or eaten my bread again. Hear me, O Ctesippus, for I am not a child anymore, and I prefer to risk death rather than see my guests treated with scorn and my handmaidens violated every night in every last corner of the house. You have a sad, ugly face, Ctesippus. It's true what they say, that wealth brings neither wisdom nor happiness."

Ctesippus lacked the courage to respond to Telemachus' threatening words. He bent back over his food and bit into a piece of meat.

I know how to play the fool when necessary. I lifted my arms into the air to get everyone's attention, showing off my rags.

"If wealth doesn't bring happiness," I said, "just imagine poverty."

Everyone started laughing and went back to their feasting.

PENELOPE

From behind a curtain at the top of the staircase I listened to the arguments during dinner, and I admired how Telemachus bravely and firmly held his own against Antinous and Ctesippus, the most vulgar of the Suitors, who thinks his vast wealth gives him the right to pursue every sort of baseness. Including being a first-rate miser.

After Telemachus' words and his threat to run Ctesippus through with the spear, a great silence fell over the hall, only the footsteps of the pantry servants bringing new baskets of food and of the handmaidens picking up the scraps thrown contemptuously to the floor by the feasters could be heard.

Finally, after a long silence, Agelaos stood up, trying to calm tempers with his words, and he began the usual hypocritical speech that I have often heard other times these last days.

"Friends," Agelaos said, "calm your tempers, try to understand Telemachus' rightful anger, and do not offend, either by word or violent deed, the foreign guest. But I would also like to say a few words for Telemachus and for Queen Penelope, now that there is no longer any hope that great Odysseus will return to us. We all know that he survived a cruel war, but he has surely perished during the long voyage home. After waiting for ten years, the only thing we can do is bow down to the will of the gods and convince our queen and young Telemachus that it is time for a new marriage. Let wise Penelope choose the most generous or the strongest or the richest among us, and let Telemachus accept the destiny that the gods have ordained for the kingdom of Ithaca."

This time, Telemachus replied with restraint, without revealing my decision to hold a competition with the bow.

"I will not be the one to forbid this marriage once my mother has made her choice. On the contrary, on that day I will offer lavish gifts and make offerings for the long-lasting peace that we all need."

His words were carefully chosen to pacify the tempers of the Suitors, but when I heard him speak about my imminent marriage, no matter how false Telemachus' promises were, a cold chill shook me down to my toes. I would have torn out all of my hair if I hadn't had the certainty that Odysseus was among us and that his presence was enough to ward off the danger announced by Agelaos. But what is Odysseus waiting for to show himself? How long is he going to keep wearing this mask? He must have a plan in mind, or is he just going to send Telemachus to certain defeat amongst these wild beasts?

All of a sudden, Theoclymenus, perhaps drunk, exploded with an unexpected string of invectives. Furious words delivered like a sinister prophesy.

"Wicked princes," he screamed, "your minds are clouded by a thick fog and your eyes unseeing and blindfolded, with no hope for light. I can already see the blood flowing in this hall and splattering the marble walls, I can already see your lacerated bodies on the ground and I hear the handmaidens' screams. The rumbles of tempests and earthquakes accompany the victims' desperate death rattles, and a dark haze blots the sky. I can read the ruin that is looming in your faces, greasy with fat. Tremble, usurpers, besieged by the shades of Erebus and chased by the ghost of vengeful Odysseus."

A moment of silence, then everyone burst into riotous laughter that shook the great hall. They called him a crazy drunkard and told him to go out into the street if all that imagined blood bothered him so much. Or maybe he was confusing the blood of the animals slaughtered for the banquets with the blood of Odysseus' impossible revenge?

Theoclymenus got up from his chair and went out into the darkness saying loudly that his mind was as clear as seawater and his legs and arms in perfect order in spite of the abundant food and wine.

It looks like Telemachus' arrival and that of the unknown guest have riled the souls of the admirers, who raise their voices at every little thing and try to placate these unexpected waves of fear with wine. They have not realized that it is Odysseus under that vagabond's clothes; nonetheless, since his arrival a strange excitement is in the air, and the desire to speed up the marriage has intensified. I thought, therefore, that this is a favorable moment for proposing the competition of the bow, having received Telemachus' consent and feeling emboldened by the secret presence of Odysseus.

I would have liked to go straight into the hall, but the banqueters had drunk too much and I was afraid that the vapors of wine might cause one of them to mistreat me and provoke an enraged reaction from Odysseus and Telemachus. My faithful Eurycleia, who overhears the words of the Suitors, has led me to understand that Telemachus' life is at stake, and it would take very little at this point to cause the violence seething in their souls to erupt against him. No matter how deplorable Odysseus' behavior has been toward me up to now, I want his vengeance to come as soon as possible, for it is my vengeance too.

I went back to my bed, putting off the official announcement of the competition until tomorrow, but I knew that I would have a hard time giving any rest to my body and my aching head. I looked at my face in the mirror and I divined new worries in the cruel thin wrinkles near my eyes and at the corners of my mouth. I hid the wrinkles with an olive oil and honey cream, and I put the mirror back into a deep wooden chest. I will not take it out again until Odysseus becomes Odysseus and Penelope becomes Penelope.

ODYSSEUS

Every evening near the end of the meal, Penelope comes down-stairs from her rooms, goes to sit in silence at the place reserved for her at the center of the great table, and feeds herself with a few small bites of meat and a glass of mead or watered-down wine. Yesterday evening she did not show her face.

Telemachus told me that she herself wishes to announce the competition of the bow, afraid that the Suitors might oppose it if the announcement were to come from him.

Penelope surely understood that the climate was not favora-ble after Ctesippus' galling actions and after Theoclymenus' speech, which I imagine was intended to punish the unbridled arrogance of the other admirers by describing a catastrophic bloodletting that seemed based precisely on my dreams of revenge. Theoclymenus looked mad, and was derided by every-one, but I know that his family, which has always raised live-stock, is famous for its steadiness and moderation, and so I find it difficult to explain his delirious prophecy. I don't know if his speech was caused by too much wine, by the news spread by Eumaios of my impending arrival, or by a premonition, as some-times happens to simple men.

But why has Penelope decided to enact the competition of the bow? For a moment I thought that she had recognized me or that the old nurse had betrayed my secret despite her solemn promise of silence, but I am now certain that my suspicions were baseless, though I continue not to trust women, be they old or young, handmaidens or queens. Telemachus' arrival, not mine, led Penelope to decide on this competition.

She certainly would have come down to the hall to make her announcement in spite of the stormy climate if she had had the merest suspicion that her husband was concealed underneath these beggar's rags. But I rule this out, because even though she has changed so much over the years, I would have noticed it if she had recognized me. Penelope may be changed, but I am still Odysseus, and my acuity never fails.

I'm trying to understand the real reasons for this competition that Penelope is going to propose to her admirers. Maybe she's hoping to ignite the rivalry between the Suitors and finally give Telemachus the chance to take the reins of his island's government. Whatever the case, it is to my advantage as well if the announcement comes at a calmer moment, and that it is neither refused nor ridiculed by the Suitors. Their tumult, their shouting, their fights, and their verbal arguments lead me to anger and confuse me when I need to keep my feelings under control and be ready to react with the speed of a thunderbolt.

Yet another restless night, interrupted like the previous one by the business of the handmaidens' lovemaking. Whisperings between the Suitors and the young women in dark corners, and sighs, and loud whimpering like dogs until dawn.

I wonder how Penelope has been able to bear this desecration of our house all this time. I'm sure she has often spied on these lust-filled movements from the staircase during her sleepless nights, and I find it hard to believe that she has been able to resist the temptation of allowing herself some furtive love affairs. This thought has tortured me since I stepped foot in my house, and the moment I close my eyes to go to sleep, my mind is filled with images that rekindle horrible suspicions and make my blood boil. There is a name for this. I am jealous. I have learned much about myself in the midst of all this turmoil, yet Penelope seems ever more enigmatic.

Every time it happens I tell myself that I have to store up
energy for my revenge and that I have to resist the temptation to
commit adultery here in my own house with a particular young
handmaiden who keeps close to me and sweet-talks me, even
though I look like a beggar. Maybe she was impressed by my
strength when I knocked Iros to the ground? There's truly no
limit to the lustful cravings of these young women, who seem to
have been hired from a brothel. And why has Penelope kept
even the most licentious handmaidens in her service? Does she
enjoy watching what she cannot have?

I'm overwhelmed not only by the arrogance and villainy of
the Suitors but also by my fate as an unhappy husband, and I
curse once again the long war of Troy that took me from my
house, and I also curse the return voyage that I myself unrea-
sonably prolonged by stopping in country after country.

After so many years, my memory of the war has become
clouded. The heroes who played a leading role fade from me
like images from a different era, and regardless of the fact that I
was their companion and shared their struggles and dangers
under the walls of the besieged city, they appear to me like a
glorious ancient age, but one with no future. Maybe the gods
want these feats, which shall never be equaled, to be recorded in
the annals of the world. Or are they destined to oblivion?

I am good at telling and weaving tales, at creating fables
about men and things, but this cannot be the task of someone
who is still suffering the consequences of that unfortunate war
and must still put his life on the line. Which feats are set in
motion by the gods anyway, and which by men?

If it is the gods who decide the good and the bad in our lives,
then what is Fate? But if it is Fate that decides for us, then of
what use are the gods?

PENELOPE

I put on my most elegant clothes, a linen cloak from Elis and a mantle the color of the sea and embroidered with gold, and I once again wore the lapis lazuli necklace that I received from Ctesippus as a partial payment for the animals killed for their feasts. Maybe I should not have accepted it, but I thought only of its value and not of the meaning that Ctesippus hoped to give it. I combed my long hair and held it in place with an ivory comb with the help of the old nurse, who has been made suspicious by the care I am dedicating to my looks, which she says is excessive.

"Why so much attention to your elegance? Who do you want to please, Penelope?"

"I cannot draw out this waiting any longer," I told her, "and thus this competition will finally give me the opportunity to choose the strongest among all my admirers."

Eurycleia looked at me, disappointed and alarmed.

"The competition sounds like a good idea to me," the old nurse said, "since I am certain that none of the Suitors will be able to string Odysseus' bow."

"No matter how strong Odysseus is, or how adept at stringing the bow," I replied, "I'm sure that the promise of a wedding will double the strength and the spirit of competition among the admirers, and thus we will put an end to what has become an unbearable wait, and to the squandering of our possessions as well."

I wanted to see whether Eurycleia would choose to betray her secret when she heard these words.

"Why did you speak of Odysseus as if he were alive and among us?"

"Odysseus is alive and among us in my memories," I replied.

The old nurse asked me, looking deep into my eyes, if something new had happened to make me take Odysseus' bow out of its case and to propose this competition.

"Exhaustion," I replied.

I'm sure that the old nurse, astounded that I still have not recognized Odysseus, would have liked to say something to me—her eyes betrayed her confusion—but she held a hand in front of her mouth to keep herself from talking. Poor, generous Eurycleia, my words have placed you in a cruel situation.

I came down to the hall just before sunset, when the house is painted by the sun's low-hanging rays and all of my admirers come together around the long table set for dinner. I halted on the final step at the bottom of the staircase and spoke forcefully and clearly.

"Your wait has gone on far too long," I said, "and since all news impels me to think with infinite sadness that I can no longer hope for Odysseus' return, I have decided to propose a competition, and to offer myself as the prize to the winner."

A murmur of surprise ran through the hall. At that moment I held up a key with an ivory handle and went to open the solid oak door that protected the bow and quiver that Odysseus had received from Iphitos, whom he had met in Messenia, where the two of them had gone to receive compensation for cattle stolen by Messenians and carried off on pirate ships. Odysseus had given Iphitos a sharp sword with an engraved golden hilt as a gift, and Iphitos returned the generosity with a powerful bow made of hard ash. With difficulty, Odysseus had managed to string the bow and shoot long, bronze-tipped arrows that passed through tree trunks and shattered stones.

I personally removed Odysseus' bow from the wall and placed it on a stool after freeing it from its leather case. Two young handmaidens placed the quiver full of arrows on the stone threshold. I then ordered that twelve axes be driven into the floor along the entire length of the great hall, in a single line and perfectly leveled.

"I remember," I said, "and perhaps some among you will remember too, how Odysseus was able to string the bow and send an arrow through the twelve rings of the axes. Using this bow requires not only muscular arms but also the strong mental determination that guides the arrow through all twelve rings. The human mind can make the air burn and break the sky in two, but I've never seen anyone strong and resolute enough to accomplish this feat, except for Odysseus. Here in front of me are young princes, strapping and well nourished. Show me, then, that you have not gone soft from all of this food and wine, and let's see if this competition can't shake your sluggish muscles to life. May each invoke his own god and force the bow to his will. Now, though, I want young Telemachus to test his strength in this competition, and if he proves able to do what his father Odysseus once did, then none of you will be allowed to compete any further."

A hum of protest rose in the hall at these words.

"You have to give us our chance," the Suitors said. "You can't start and finish the competition all at once. Is this what we have waited for so long? And if Telemachus wins, will you choose to marry your son?"

But I quickly replied.

"This period of waiting has been rich with pleasures of food and lust alike for you, and so you have no cause for complaint, while for many years I have suffered a widowhood made more pitiable by its uncertainty. Aside from spurious rumors, we still know nothing about Odysseus, but if he has not come back after a ten-year voyage, this may mean that he has perished in an accident at sea or on land, or that it is a scant desire to return that has kept him far from his homeland and his wife. Should this be the case, then Odysseus deserves to have me end my sacrifice and start a new family. But as queen and mother, I cannot betray Telemachus' legitimate rights. Therefore, if he is strong enough and skillful enough to equal his father, then it is only right that the palace be cleared of all of you and Telemachus remain the sole ruler of the island."

A clamor of comments rose from the Suitors, but none dared to impede Telemachus' attempt. They didn't want to offend Penelope, but deep down they were calmed by the conviction that a young man with such a wiry physique would never be able to string Odysseus' bow. The handmaidens placed the bow and quiver in front of Telemachus, who removed the mantle from his shoulders and prepared for the challenge. Before starting the competition, he chose to lecture all of the Suitors seated on their stools, waiting impatiently.

"The moment of truth is upon us. If you truly burn with honest desire for the queen my mother, and you are not here just for feasting, call upon your strength and do not back out of the competition if my own attempt fails."

At this, Telemachus planted his feet firmly on the stone threshold and took the bow in his hands under the gaze of the speechless Suitors. In the silence of the great hall, thrice did he use all his strength to string the powerful bow, which nevertheless resisted all his efforts. At the fourth try, Telemachus bent the bow against his knee, but noticed that Odysseus' eyes were signaling him to give up.

"Alas," Telemachus said, "my strength is not enough to equal my father Odysseus. I don't know if I can blame my youthful age or if I will never be able to use this bow to protect myself from the insults thrown in my face. Without the help of strong arms, the heart is not enough. It is now your turn to prove your strength under the watchful eyes of queen Penelope."

And he hung Odysseus' bow on a hook on the wall and laid the quiver on the ground.

ODYSSEUS

In her speech to the Suitors, Penelope spoke of my scant desire to return to my homeland. Only now do I begin to understand how full her heart is of resentment over the long, too long years of my return voyage, and in light of this, her announcement of the competition of the bow makes sense. I can't blame her, even if her words threw me into dismay and filled my chest with a bitterness that will not be helpful when my turn in the competition comes to bend the bow and then battle the horde of Suitors.

I have not held this superb weapon in twenty years, and now my forehead is burning with the worry that I might not be equal to the test. A failed attempt would drag me into shame in front of the Suitors and Penelope. If that should happen, I would leave on a new voyage to find a new homeland, or go back to wandering from one land to another as I did after the fall of Troy.

This is the first time I have felt that bold self-assurance that distinguishes and steadies even the dumbest of warriors slip away from me. The true heroes, Achilles, Hector, Agamemnon, never lost that blind faith in their strength even for an instant, and doubt never once insinuated itself in their minds. Unlike them, I have always doubted everything, and that doubt always helped me understand and be victorious, but since arriving under the skies of Ithaca, there have truly been too many doubts torturing me, as if I had landed on an island of uncertainty and ever-falling tears.

"Each of us will come to the stone threshold, one after another, starting from the right."

So ordered Antinous, who with these words took control of the competition as if he were master of the house, as if he already could rely on Penelope's favors. She stayed in her seat, as still and silent as a statue, her gaze distant and empty.

I watched her carefully, hoping to catch her uncertain or worried, but instead I caught, suddenly on her lips, a smile, which again made me uncomfortable. What was the meaning of that smile, what thoughts did it reveal? What secret confidence allowed her to smile at a moment of such great tension? Maybe she suggested the competition knowing full well who would be the winner? There can't be any trickery, for Telemachus himself tried the bow unsuccessfully. But maybe she slipped the key to the cabinet where the bow was kept to one of the Suitors in advance, so he would be able to practice? Maybe she cut a deal with Antinous, who I noticed was quite calm, as if he were already the winner? Or was she counting on this strategy and the failure of the competition to put an end to the presence of her admirers in the palace? Penelope's gaze was distant, as if everything happening had nothing to do with her. How could I have hoped that her gaze would settle on this old vagabond covered in rags? How can I even complain since it was I myself who decided to keep her in the dark about this entire charade?

The first to stand up was Leodes, son of Oinops, the most restrained of the Suitors, who according to Eumaios had more than once tried to temper the gluttony and haughtiness of his companions. He walked quickly to the stone threshold and immediately grabbed the limb of the bow, trying hard to bend it and attach the bowstring. With all his strength he tried twice, to no avail, and with a dismayed gesture hung the bow on the wall hook.

"I cannot string Odysseus' bow," he exclaimed, "so let another of you take it up. But if you hope to conquer Penelope with this bow, get ready to court another woman somewhere else, for you will be unable to bend this weapon, and I tell you that this competition will bring you nothing but embarrassment."

Leodes' words instantly provoked Antinous' anger.

"Don't blame the others, Leodes, if your mother gave birth to a worthless archer. Soon enough you will see others among your companions who are able to string the bow and send the arrow through the twelve rings. It is a sign of cowardice to ascribe your own weaknesses to others, and it would have been better for your dignity if you had just shut up."

Following this harsh rebuke from Antinous, Eurymachus came forward and ordered the goatherd Melanthius to stoke the fire, lay sheepskins on a stool in front of the fireplace, and place on top of the skins a large piece of fat that began to melt from the heat of the flames. The young men getting ready for the competition then requested that the warm, greasy skins be wrapped around the limb of the bow to make it more flexible.

While Melanthius warmed the limb of the bow, I watched Penelope, who looked absent, almost bored by the delay. A very strange attitude before a competition that was to decide her future.

Dozens and dozens of Suitors, one after another, took their turns at the stone threshold and tried to string the bow that had been warmed with the fat-soaked skins. But every time, they failed in shame, and some of them returned to their seats muttering curses against the gods.

I watched the competition in silence and delighted in the ineptitude of these young admirers who contorted their straining bodies, their veins popping in their necks and their mouths twisting. Then cross-eyed Amphimedon's turn came, and he mounted the stone threshold and grabbed the bow. But Eurymachus stopped him immediately.

"If you ever proved able to string the bow, I would run from the hall, because there's no knowing where the arrow would end up."

A smattering of laughter in the hall. Amphimedon, offended, threw the bow to the ground and returned to his seat.

But my attention, like Penelope's, was focused on Antinous and Eurymachus, the strongest and haughtiest of all the Suitors.

I slowly got up from my seat and nodded my head toward Eumaios and the loyal oxherd Philoetius to follow me, as if I wanted to distance myself from the pitiful show of the Suitors trying to bend the inflexible bow. Outside, I spoke a few quick words to the two herdsmen.

"Would you be ready to fight," I asked, "against these arrogant admirers if powerful Odysseus were suddenly to arrive amongst us to take his revenge, as would be right after all of the offenses he has received? Or would he find you allied with the side of the admirers? What does your heart tell you? What would you choose?"

With no hesitation the two herdsmen replied that their arms would become doubly strong if a generous god made Odysseus, their lord and master, appear before their eyes.

"But the gods don't give their favors to two poor herdsmen," Philoetius said humbly.

"And yet here I am," I said to the two loyal herdsmen. "It is I, Odysseus, hidden beneath this ragged cloak, here in my land after twenty years of hardship, but still as solid as well-tempered iron."

I showed them the scar left from the deep wound that I received from the wild boar on that distant day during the hunt on Mount Helicon, a wound that they both knew well, having been present during the incident.

Eumaios and Philoetius were speechless with amazement, and their eyes filled with tears.

"This is no time for crying," I said, to avoid the embarrassment of my own emotions in front of the two herdsmen.

What would they have thought of their king Odysseus if they had seen him break down in tears? I plucked them up with a gesture and spoke a few more words.

"When you return to the hall, make sure to block all of the doors with solid bolts so that none of the Suitors can get away. But first, have the handmaidens leave, for this will be no sight for their eyes. And speak to no one about my presence, not even Penelope, until you get an order from me personally."

The two herdsmen swore, with tears running down their faces, that they would be at my side until vengeance was served. They took my hands and covered them with kisses, wetting them with tears as salty as the sea. There's nothing but crying on this island, I thought, and at a time when it would be best to keep our eyes dry and wary.

"I'm going back in now," I said to them, "so that no one will see us together here outside, especially that vile spy Iros. Follow after me in a little while, and when Telemachus asks for it, you, Eumaios, will hand me the bow and arrows."

I went back into the hall and saw Eurymachus warming the limb of the bow directly over the flames of the fireplace. He then took his place on the stone threshold and tried to string the bow

in order to shoot an arrow. His face became red and sweaty from
the strain, his neck as tense and rigid as the trunk of an oak tree,
the veins standing out on his forehead; after the second failed
attempt, he quickly gave up, lowering his face in humiliation
and throwing the bow to the ground. He spoke to his companions sitting in the hall.

"I am driven to despair," he said in a broken voice, "not only
because a wedding with the beautiful and honest queen Penelope has eluded me, but because our shame will be told to the
children of our children for many long years. After my failure, I
know that none of us will be able to string Odysseus' bow."

"Speak for yourself and not for others," Antinous scolded,
saying that it was now time to start drinking again and to
complete the competition the following day after a good night's
rest.

"Let the servants make the wine flow, and tomorrow the gods
will give strength to whomever they please, but we won't abandon hard-hearted Penelope's competition so easily. It is to her
that we must prove we are no less than Odysseus, not only to
ourselves."

While the Suitors, encouraged by Antinous' words, started
drinking wine again from the silver goblets, I stood up from my
seat and stamped my feet in order to get the attention of the
entire hall.

"I'd like to say a few words to you admirers, but in particular
I apply to Eurymachus and Antinous so that they will give me
the chance to test my own strength and see if a vagabond's life
and struggles have weakened me, or if I still retain a few sparks
of my former vigor."

"What wild idea is running through your wretched mind,
foreigner?" Antinous reproached me. "We accepted your ragged,

lice-filled body at our noble table upon Telemachus' insistence, but now the wine vapors have so shaken your reason that they induce you to ask for that which is not yours and to offend the rank that allows each of us to propose ourselves as husband to Queen Penelope."

Penelope immediately intervened in a loud, grave voice.

"Antinous, it is not right to offend Telemachus' guest. Or perhaps you are afraid that if he is able to string the bow and send the arrow through the twelve rings, he will have me as his wife and take Odysseus' place as ruler of the island? Or do you all think he wants to carry me off like Paris carried off Helen, even though you know full well that he doesn't even have a roof to protect him from the rain? I don't think our guest has such intentions, only that he wants to test his strength, like in a palaestra. As for the rest, you have nothing to fear, so remain in your seats and let's see what this foreigner can do, and if he cannot bend the bow, you can make as much fun of him as you want, though if he wins the competition, he will have earned greater respect and an end to the ridicule he has been subjected to."

"We have no fear that he will carry you off as his bride, generous Penelope, or that he hopes to become king of Ithaca," Antinous replied, "but rather that the story of how a poor beggar of no rank was able to string Odysseus' bow after the noble admirers had to give up the exploit in shame will be told across the entire island and the entire black continent. This infamous tale would be told for many centuries, to the children of our children as Eurymachus said, and our legacy would be dragged through the mud. This is the only thing we fear, generous Penelope."

Poor Antinous, in his arrogance he was still thinking that in the distant future some lazy singer would bother to resuscitate his name and the deeds of this little island of Ithaca, lost in the

great ocean. Quite the opposite. In just a few years, even the
Trojan War will be forgotten, even though it seemed worthy of
being written in the annals of history, at least to those of us who
fought in it. Men have so many illusions about the future movements of time, and they don't understand that their memorable
feats will be forgotten as quickly as the rivalries between columns of ants. Wretched Antinous, to worry about his legacy in
the world when he doesn't know that he himself is soon to be
erased from this life.

"Give him the bow and let's see what he can do," Penelope
said gravely. "It seems that our guest is a man of noble stock in
spite of his looks, so if he manages to shoot an arrow it will be of
no dishonor to any of you princely admirers. And if by some
chance he wins the competition, he will receive from my own
hands a luxurious cloak and tunic, a shining bronze spear, a
sharp sword, and sturdy leather boots, since he will no doubt
wish to continue on with his voyages. We all know that when a
man gets a taste for adventure and travels vast parts of the earth
and sea, the voyages that began out of necessity turn into a kind
of bondage and craving. No one will ever be able to make him
stay in one place and he will continue wandering the rest of his
life, forgetting about his family, his friends, his loved ones, and
his possessions. And should he ever return home he would be
incapable of embracing those emotions that were previously
more precious to him than gold. This is why among the gifts he
shall receive from Penelope, should he win the competition, I
have included a pair of well-made leather boots, cinched by a
bronze buckle, fire-branded, and sewn with cord that has been
soaked in pitch."

Ah-ha! I said to myself, Penelope is speaking to Odysseus'
ghost. How much bitterness and resentment are in her words.

Now I understand why she proposed this competition. After so many years of waiting, she can still weep a few tears, but Odysseus has disappeared from her horizon. If I allowed myself to be drawn along by the capricious waves of adventure instead of taking the straight route home to Ithaca, perhaps it was precisely because I was secretly afraid that Penelope's feelings might have changed, and that the day of our reunion would have been too bitter for me. And now, under the artifice of this disguise, I am bringing myself closer to this cruel truth.

Am I foundering in my native land, in my very home?

PENELOPE

I hope I wasn't overly explicit when I spoke about wandering in distant lands as an execrable vice that makes you forget your home and your loved ones. The words leapt forth from my heart, honest and painful. They were directed at him, but Odysseus, wrapped in his rags, didn't bat an eyelid or twist his lips or crease his brow. He is as hard as stone and impassable, even when facing an event like the competition of the bow, which I thought would have stirred distant and happy memories for him.

Telemachus, meanwhile, speaking about Odysseus as if he truly were a wandering foreigner, says that he has shed salty tears more than once when remembering his home in Crete and the wife that he has not seen for twenty years. Telemachus was trying his best to tell me that other veterans of the Trojan War had traveled the world for many years and yet had remained true in their hearts to their homes. I think he charitably wanted to justify his father's masquerade, and at the same time prepare me for the moment when Odysseus will drop the mask. How good Telemachus has become at telling lies, and how much he resembles his father even in his bad habits.

Naturally, I keep putting up with all of their lies, but in the meantime I will order a pair of boots from an expert cobbler, which I will give to Odysseus at the right moment, and I will tell him to start wandering again with lightened feet across the lands of the earth, or to unfurl his sails on the boundless seas, and to undertake all of the adventures he has proved to have such a dogged penchant for. How many things must I forgive Odysseus. He is a born liar and master of trickery, and this can even be a good thing when the lies and tricks are used against Trojan enemies or anyone who tries to block his way, but it is a desperate and unpardonable infamy when he decides to use these means against his wife. I have lived through so much disappointment under the roof of this house, and a new disappointment is now added to the old ones.

Let the competition continue, then. The challenge is now between Antinous and Odysseus, and I will have to keep my word and give myself to the stronger of the two. Either accept Antinous as Odysseus' replacement and as sole ruler of this palace in the unfortunate case that he wins the competition, or take my place once again at the side of beloved Odysseus, even though his current behavior has done more to drive us apart than a twenty-year absence.

Every night I have dreamed of embracing his body, as hard as bronze, and of kissing his war scars one by one, but when I need to, I can control my emotions and punish his arrogance. If Odysseus wants to win me back, it will be a much more difficult siege than the one of Troy many years ago with the Achaeans.

Telemachus stepped in and said that it was not up to me whether the competition should continue, but that it was his

decision to make. It pleases me to see Telemachus showing authority, even if it is against me.

"Go into your rooms, mother," he said, "and let the men in
this house decide what should and should not be done."

I didn't react against Telemachus' decision, even if his ways
were ruder than they should have been. So I went up to my
rooms, though I was quite determined not to remain locked up
at a moment like this one, since the true protagonist of this competition is me. Neither Odysseus nor Telemachus will be able to
push me into the background the way they are trying to.

I have eyes to see and ears to hear, and so, as I have done
many other times on less noble occasions, I will hide behind the
curtain at the top of the stairs and from there I will learn what is
going on down below in the great hall.

Upon entering my rooms I looked up toward the pale moon
that I have turned to on so many interminable nights. I am tired
of everything that happens in this house. Over all these years of
waiting, how many thoughts, how much sadness and loneliness
have evaporated into the sky between my rooms and the moon
high above. And now the moon, which makes the plants and the
sea grow, is cold and silent, hiding itself behind the moving
clouds and ignoring my pain. And something dies within me,
every day.

I feel like an empty shell, it's true, but should I give in now,
just when Odysseus is about to take hold of the bow and a solution may finally be within grasp? But what will happen when the
competition begins anew? Will Odysseus, after twenty years
wasted on useless, exhausting adventures, be able to bend the
bow as before? No, I can't let myself lose heart in these weari-
some regrets about the past; I must simply stand behind this
curtain and watch the events that happen downstairs in the

crowded great hall, where my destiny, and that of Ithaca, is to be decided.

ODYSSEUS

As soon as I had the bow in my hands I stroked it like a musician strokes his cithara, or a sailor handles the helm of a ship before untying it from its moorings. I checked to see if the white ash wood had any woodworm holes, and if the metal supports were well fastened, then I wiped the limb on my cloak to clean away the grease. Finally, I spit on the palms of my hands and grabbed the two metallic ends of the bow, tested its resistance twice, and then, at last, with a strong swift motion, I bent the wood to string the bow.

A buzz of amazement rose from the hall. I turned my gaze around and, in a show of defiance, plucked the cord, which let out a festive and vibrant sound, though it was gloomy to the Suitors, who remained frozen and silent.

The youngest among them watched me in dismay, for they had understood that this was not the first time I had held that object in my hands, and that I would use it with a prowess worthy of Odysseus.

I plucked the cord again when the Suitors began to show signs of impatience.

"That's a bow in your hands, not a cithara!" Antinous yelled furiously. And the others joined in his exclamations of protest.

So I slowly dropped my ragged cloak to the floor, then I took an arrow from the quiver, preparing to shoot. But once again I stopped myself, with the arrow in my hand, creating greater tension in the hall.

I stared through the twelve rings lined in a row, then I filled my chest with a deep breath. I remember how once, when the shot was perfect, the arrow didn't even graze a single ring of the axes.

"Come on, let's see what you can do, beggar!"

I finally pulled the cord back firmly, bending the limb of the bow, took aim, and sent the arrow whistling through all twelve rings of the axes. It smashed into the marble wall at the back of the hall in a shower of sparks.

A buzz of alarm ran through the hall from one end to the other, and again a deathly silence settled as I began speaking to Telemachus.

"The guest whom you have generously welcomed into your palace and allowed to participate in the competition has not dishonored you, Telemachus. The bow bent easily in my hands and the arrow flew in the correct direction. This is my answer to the insults from the Suitors, who now regard me with the respect that I have deservedly earned, even though they would still like to chase me from this house, as if it were theirs. From now on, I will have a regular place at the royal meals," I said, turning toward the Suitors, speechless from their surprise, "and with every right, because I am no usurper like you. Sit down to your food and wine, which are your most pressing concerns and all you can think about, and soothe your astonished souls with music for just a while longer. If a cithara and a song and the smell of roasted meat are not enough to chase away your fears, I will do so with this bow and these arrows.

I removed the beggar's rags that still covered my chest and spoke loudly and menacingly.

"The party's over, and the twelve rings of the axes will not be the next target for my arrows."

With these words I let fly an arrow that struck Antinous in the throat just as he was lifting his silver goblet full of wine.

With a death rattle, Antinous crashed to the floor while a gush of blood shot from the wound and his mouth. The chalice full of wine fell to the ground, as well as the food he had been about to eat.

The shocked Suitors crouched behind columns and in the corners of the hall and looked about for the weapons that Telemachus and I had wisely hidden.

"You have killed the strongest and most noble young man of Ithaca, and this crime will be your death sentence," Ctesippus yelled from behind a column.

"Why are you hiding? Where is your arrogance now? Where is your pride now?" I said to all the Suitors. "You prayed for my death and slaughtered my herds, seduced my handmaidens and shamelessly courted my wife, and now you must die like dogs to pay once and for all for your disgraceful actions."

The Suitors were all shaking like leaves in terror, having finally understood who I was.

Eurymachus alone showed enough courage to answer me.

"If you are truly Odysseus, I will admit that you have many reasons to be angry. But now Antinous is dead, he who more than anyone was responsible for these evils. He was the one who urged us on, not merely because he thought he was Penelope's favorite, but because he was evil-spirited and was plotting to kill Telemachus and become king of Ithaca. We now ask your forgiveness, and with gold and cattle we are prepared to settle our debts for everything we have consumed over these years."

And so I have confirmation that Antinous was Penelope's favorite. This is what Eurymachus has declared with cowardly impudence. I know very well how easy it is to lie, and so I will later uncover the extent to which his statement is true by reading Penelope's eyes. Lying comes easily to me, and it is equally easy for me to unravel other people's falsehoods. Eyes don't lie. But now, I had to hurry up with my revenge before the Suitors were able to organize any defense, or use their strength or the help of some handmaiden to escape.

"Not even if you paid me down to your very last coin, or that of your fathers," I yelled, "would you be able to stop me. I only regret that I will dirty the walls of this house with your impure blood, but I will be overjoyed to personally find someone to wash the walls and painters to redo the decorations once I have finished taking my revenge."

The Suitors watched me in terror from the corners of the great hall and behind the overturned tables where they had taken shelter, while the more intelligent of them checked the locks on the doors to try to open an escape route.

"Well, then, now that clemency has been rejected and our generous offer of repayment has been refused," Eurymachus yelled, "unsheathe your daggers and let's confront this haughty Odysseus all together."

Eurymachus was the first to launch himself at me, but I hit him quickly in the chest with a fatal arrow. After him, Amphinomus leapt up, about to strike me with his dagger, but Telemachus caught him from behind with a spear thrust that sent him sprawling to the ground. Striking his brow on a stone step, his head bounced with a dull thud, like a pumpkin.

"Run to get the weapons in the storeroom now," I said to Telemachus, "because there are not enough arrows. I will defend myself with the help of the two herdsmen for the moment."

Eumaios and Philoetius defended me at my side, cutting down the advancing Suitors with their swords. They fought with élan and fury, almost with joy, my two faithful herdsmen.

Using the weapons Telemachus brought back, the massacre continued. The Suitors fell one after another with their eyes wide in terror and their mouths horribly contorted. But then the goatherd Melanthius ran to the storeroom, which Telemachus had left open, and carried back a dozen spears and shields for the Suitors, returning at a run to the storeroom to get even more weapons.

"Run, Eumaios," I urged the herdsman, "and punish Melanthius, who has put our lives in danger with these weapons."

Eumaios surprised Melanthius from behind while he was collecting other weapons and knocked him flat with a blow to his nape. Then he tied his arms and legs in a knot and hung him from a hook on the beam overhead.

"You can keep watch from your perch here until you have taken your last breath—that way you'll have enough time to repent for all the wicked services you performed for the Suitors during Odysseus' absence."

Melanthius wailed and cried for mercy, but Eumaios, after gathering more weapons, closed the door of the storeroom, leaving him hanging from the beam like a pig for slaughter.

PENELOPE

The gulls are screeching so loudly and flying so low around the palace that my eyes can barely follow them. These stupid seabirds descend, almost brushing against the roof, then zoom back up to practically disappear in the sky, and then they descend again, and as they get closer their din becomes more and more piercing.

It is not unusual to have the noisy presence of seagulls in the sky above Ithaca, but today their cries sound sharper than usual, as if they have sensed in the air that something terrible is happening in the palace.

The gulls finally flew off, and only one of them was left hovering motionless in the air, screeching funereal cries as if it wanted to tell me something. Can seagulls smell the odor of blood? What I saw from behind the curtain threw me into distress. What horror and pity, poor haughty Antinous. And you, fly away, stupid seagull, and make no more noise where men are dying.

I could never even bear the blood of the butchered oxen for the banquets, and I could spend the rest of my life without eating meat rather than watch those poor animals killed. And yet I watched something so much more horrible and cruel when the arrow pierced young Antinous' neck and the blood gushed from the mouth of that unfortunate soul. A haughty and vigorous man was reduced to a poor lifeless body in a few moments. That's how cruel death comes.

This is the first time I have watched a man being killed. I stood there for a long time with a great emptiness in my mind, no thoughts, no emotions. I would have liked to cry, but my eyes were as dry as ashes.

I have held my own against my admirers' arrogance for many years, and over the past few days I have feared for Telemachus' life. I used every method I could to try to convince them to stop consuming Odysseus' possessions, and when I saw that they indifferently continued to stuff their filthy faces, I felt contempt for them down to the bottom of my soul. But now that they are squealing like maddened goats as they fall under Odysseus and Telemachus' mortal blows, they inspire infinite pity.

New, terrifying screams from the Suitors led me back to my place behind the curtain. A savage scene. Blood everywhere, on the walls, on the floor, on the food fallen to the ground during the massacre. I saw the floor covered with horribly wounded corpses, like animals after a hunt. And I heard Odysseus shout as he raced from one side of the hall to the other, roused by all that blood.

A group of survivors led by Agelaos, who urged them on, made a final rush against Odysseus and Telemachus and the two herdsmen, who defended and attacked as they could. I had felt pity for the killed Suitors, but now I trembled over the fate of Odysseus and Telemachus, who avoided as best they could the spears of the infuriated Suitors, and who struck back with a superhuman, insane energy.

I have heard war spoken of as a heroic enterprise, and the illustrious feats of warriors who distinguish themselves in bravery are celebrated, but all this blood . . . how offensive to humanity, what a horror against nature. What is heroism if not the glorification of violence? Once I saw two dogs who tore each other apart bloodily in a furious fight. I had been shocked by that violence, but now I have seen that man is the cruelest and most violent of all the earth's creatures.

I watched Demoptolemus, Euryades, and Peisander fall bloodily to the ground. In the melee, Telemachus was wounded on one hand, but Odysseus continued the battle with his wounded son and the two herdsmen, and under their mortal blows fell Eurydamas, Amphimedon, Polybus, and the arrogant Ctesippus, to whom the herdsman Eumaios spoke as he lay dying.

"This," he said, kicking him in the face, "is your reward for throwing that ox hoof at Odysseus when he was begging in the hall."

But Ctesippus could not hear those words, for his body was already lifeless, torn out on the ground.

I know that men are cruel in war and that when we speak of a hero whom everyone fears and admires we really mean a ruthless man who takes the lives of other men by making their blood spray. This is a hero? And is Odysseus any different from the others?

I saw the diviner Leodes approach them and embrace their knees, supplicating.

"I beg you, divine Odysseus, to have pity on my life. Anyone can tell you that I always tried to restrain the Suitors and I never even offended your handmaidens. It is not fair for me to die together with those who acted with such infamy."

And Odysseus replied haughtily:

"If you were the diviner for the Suitors, you surely must have made offerings against my return, or for me to be killed by the tempestuous ocean. You too will have prayed for my wife to fall into the arms of her admirers, and for this, you shall not escape death."

At the last of these hard-hearted words, Odysseus grabbed a sword and in a single blow cut through his neck. Leodes' head rolled to the ground while his lips were still moving, mouthing words of supplication. This is the hero who has occupied my every thought for twenty long years?

I never could have imagined that such a massacre could take place right in my house and in front of my very eyes. Now I understand the cries of the gulls sailing in the sky above the palace. Even these stupid seabirds rebel against so much blood. I should probably celebrate the fact that Odysseus has come to take revenge for the wrongs that he incurred when the hope that he was still alive was as tenuous as a spiderweb. But what joy can there be surrounded by all this blood?

When Telemachus returned from Sparta, he came to tell us that Odysseus was finally sailing toward Ithaca, on the seas of

Ithaca. Stupid Suitors, who instead of fixing their eyes on the horizon took the news as nothing more than a pitiful attempt to frighten them, and redoubled their arrogance. And now inexorable revenge has arrived, and they are being butchered one after another like beasts led to slaughter.

I saw faithful Mentor climb up to the loft and crouch down like a hen in order to escape the massacre, without lifting even a finger to help his beloved Odysseus and Telemachus. Should I thus decide that he, with all his wisdom, is a lesser man than the uncouth swineherd Eumaios and cowherd Philoetius, who took up spears and shields to fight side-by-side with Odysseus and Telemachus?

Odysseus spared the singer Terpiade's life, who had hurried to embrace his knees, placing his golden cithara at his feet and supplicating him with tears.

"My only fault," he said, "is to have sung during their banquets for a modest payment that allowed me one meal a day and a few woolen clothes. The gods protect singing, and you, Odysseus, will show mercy for a singer who always performed his sacrifices to the gods and who has kept your illustrious name alive in his memory."

Telemachus intervened too, and implored his father to spare him, because singing can bear no blame and Terpiade was never in a position to deny the Suitors' requests.

Seeing that Odysseus spared the singer, the herald Medon also came out from the corner of the hall where he had been hiding, went up to Telemachus, and begged him to intercede on his behalf to Odysseus. And so these two poor men saved themselves.

A door was opened at Telemachus' order so that Terpiade and Medon could go outside and give thanks to the gods with an abundant sacrifice. The smoke from roasting meat arrives all the way to the top of Olympus, tickles the nostrils of the gods, and inclines them to be kindhearted.

I hope that they will be kindhearted with Odysseus in spite of the blood he has spilled, and that they lead him to mend his ways after the atrocious offense he has committed in showing such mistrust toward his wife.

ODYSSEUS

When old Eurycleia, called by Telemachus, came into the corpse-filled hall and saw me covered in blood like a savage beast who has mauled and killed another beast, she let out a shout of joy and ran to hug me, unconcerned about dirtying her pure white clothes with blood.

"Contain your joy," I told her, "for it is not right to celebrate the death of others. Since I arrived secretly on my island, too many things have made me suffer and continue to fill my heart with bitterness and my eyes with salty tears. Send a man to the roof to remove a tile so that the spirits of the dead can leave freely."

"With all these corpses we'll need to uncover the entire roof," Eurycleia replied.

"And now you will call here into the hall all of the handmaidens who gave their bodies to the Suitors and disrespected Penelope and her house. Out of fifty handmaidens I have been told that only a dozen have soiled themselves with ignoble acts. You will order them to carry the corpses from the hall, to wash the blood from every object, wall, floor, and table, and to scrub every surface with a sponge until not a trace of blood remains."

"I will have the Suitors' corpses carried outside in the open air," said Eurycleia, "where their evil spirits can fly away faster."

I then called the two herdsmen.

"When they have finished cleaning everything," I said, "lead all twelve of the treacherous handmaidens into the courtyard and with your sharp swords send them quickly to Hades so they can reunite with their gluttonous and lecherous lovers down there in the dark."

Telemachus objected, though, that death by sword seemed too kind for those wretches who had offended Penelope and himself, and who had turned the palace into a brothel. And so he had a thick rope strung from a column to a hook in the wall of the courtyard. The handmaidens, kicking their feet, were hanged one after the other with a hemp cord around their necks, and they stopped breathing and left this world in which they were no longer worthy of living. The last one to be hanged, so that she would have to watch all the others, was Melantho, the Suitors' spy and enemy of Penelope.

But this was not enough for Eumaios and Philoetius, thirsting for vengeance. They took Melanthius, whose hands were tied to his feet but who was still breathing, and they cut off his nose and ears, heedless of his desperate cries, and then tore off his member and threw it to the dogs to eat. But they sniffed that bloody food, already covered in flies, and left it there on the ground like infected meat.

The two herdsmen had old grudges with the goatherd Melanthius. Melanthius, servant and spy to the Suitors, had received praise and many gifts for the animals that he brought to the palace, even golden objects that the princes had filched from among the furnishings. And he had laid claim to all of the horns of the slaughtered animals and sold them to the Phoenician merchants.

The two herdsmen's vengeance had exploded like a violent storm and bloody fury that needed to take instant revenge for all the wrongs they had suffered and the offenses to their ruler. Such deep wounds can be assuaged only by blood, which now trickled down the polished stones of the courtyard where all of the victims' bodies had been carried, and over which a swarm of flies was buzzing.

I asked old Eurycleia to purify the floor, the walls, and the columns of the great hall with burning sulfur. As the faithful handmaidens arrived from every corner, I embraced them and gave them tender caresses, and Eurycleia immediately instructed them to put everything back in place. And so I watched the resurrection of the palace to its original, shining beauty, bit by bit.

My eyes filled with tears again, and I quickly went into the courtyard so that the handmaidens would not see their honorable king Odysseus crying.

PENELOPE

The old nurse came to finally announce with heartfelt words that the beggar who had arrived from distant lands, the author of the massacre of the admirers, was none other than my husband Odysseus, disguised in order to sneak into his house and carry out his revenge.

"A belated announcement," she added, "since words are unnecessary when facts speak for themselves."

"I have no idea, Eurycleia, why you would come here to make fun of your queen," I said, pretending to be furious. "The gods are capricious and can make a wise woman, as you have always been, go crazy and make you play a horrible joke even when my heart is in pieces because of the massacre that has bloodied my house. I have suffered over my beloved Odysseus' absence for many years, but it was certainly not with all this blood that I would have liked to erase the disrespect of my admirers. You know how I loathed the Trojan War, which took so many men from their families, and you know how I even asked you to break Odysseus' leg with an ax handle just to keep him from leaving. Unfortunately you refused to obey my order then, and I wasn't brave enough to do it myself. Many died in that distant war, and others who survived the war had to face tragic destinies. I've heard that when Agamemnon returned home he was killed by his cheating wife Clytemnestra and her lover Aegisthus. Others wandered the seas and perished in the raging waves. Now you come to salt my open wound, and it is only out of respect for your loyalty and your old age that I don't send you away with the insults that any other handmaiden would have deserved."

Eurycleia opened her eyes wide in amazement.

"I would never dare make fun of you, my most beloved queen, by speaking lightly about what pains you so cruelly. How can you believe that I would come to renew your pain if I weren't certain of what I say? The beggar whom everyone offended for his looks and the rags he hid beneath has now dropped his mask and revealed himself as Odysseus. Telemachus already knew this and they secretly planned to eliminate all of your violent admirers. They hid the weapons and locked the doors to the great hall and armed the two faithful herdsmen without whom they would not have been able to fight the multitude of Suitors. Of all the handmaidens only I had discovered his presence when, during the sacred washing of his feet, I recognized the thick scar that a wild boar had engraved on his leg during a hunt, as you well remember. But he demanded my silence and I obeyed my lord. Only now can I speak openly."

I replied without raising my voice, but quite firmly:

"If you think that the scar on his leg is proof, I counter by saying that many wild boars have attacked and wounded many hunters, leaving behind thick scars. A wound to the leg, you say, but
where else would an enraged boar wound a hunter? And how can
I believe your words, sweet, innocent Eurycleia, how can I
believe that after twenty years of separation, finding himself in
the vicinity of his wife, Odysseus never showed a single sign that
betrayed his feelings? How can I believe that he planned a difficult and dangerous vendetta without telling me a single word? I
am absolutely certain that Odysseus, as I remember him, would
have told me everything and that if secrecy was needed he knows
perfectly well that Penelope can keep a secret in her heart as if it
were at the bottom of a deep well. Only a stranger could harbor
such mistrust toward me, not Odysseus. Never."

For a few moments wise old Eurycleia remained speechless.
She herself had no idea how to justify Odysseus' arrogant mistrust of me.

"You know the mortal risk that Odysseus faced in confronting the savage crowd of your admirers and that a single word
could have compromised his plans and placed his life and that of
Telemachus in danger. Or perhaps you are afraid that someone
might treacherously take revenge against the both of you if you
take Odysseus back in your arms? I'm having trouble following
your thoughts and suspicions, but I can reassure you about that,
for I am certain that none of the Suitors escaped the swords of
Odysseus and Telemachus and that all of them are lying bloody,
and the faithful handmaidens are spreading sulfur everywhere
to purify the great banquet hall of their blood. Odysseus is
seated in front of the fireplace and is waiting anxiously for you
to come downstairs and embrace him now that vengeance is
served and you are once again free from your admirers' siege.

"The gods do not tolerate offenses and iniquity," I told Eurycleia, "and thus they must have wisely guided the hand of this stranger. A powerful and astute man is this foreigner, but he himself said that by winning the competition he had no intention of winning my hand. Could such words have ever come from Odysseus' lips?"

These words forced Eurycleia into a new silence, surprised by how confident I was that Odysseus could not be the stranger who massacred the Suitors.

"You speak of a powerful, astute man, my dear Penelope," the old nurse replied, "but who on this earth is more powerful and astute than Odysseus? Who could have bent the bow and shot the arrow through twelve rings and then sent one after another of the strong young admirers to their deaths? I see that my words haven't convinced you and I don't want to take offense even if I have every right to, but the facts that I have recounted and that I know you saw yourself from behind the curtain should be enough to convince you. I understand how your heart has become as hard as stone during the many years of waiting, but now you must let go of your reticence, you must place your trust in a positive destiny, because if in your pride you reject the grace that the gods are offering to you on a golden platter, you would be gravely offending their ultimate authority and goodwill."

I admit that Eurycleia's heartfelt words were painful to my ears, but my wounded pride dictated every word that came from my lips.

"I have to get rid of many negative thoughts before I can come down to the hall; I have to peel my eyes away from this sky that is confounding me with all these birds flying around the house, screeching. Your words have not removed my doubts about this violent and brave foreigner who proved able not only to string Odysseus' bow but to face and kill, with the help of Telemachus and the two herdsmen, all of the young Suitors who had taken up residence in my house. I can, if you wish, admire his bravery and, as promised, reward him with a mantle and tunic and well-made boots so he can return to his wandering ways. But ask no more of me. I must even praise Telemachus for knowing how to choose a formidable ally in order to take back everything that had insolently been taken away from him, but you cannot expect me to accept this foreign wanderer as my husband just because he killed off all the other admirers. Should I contradict his own words after he declared he had no intention of marrying me? I'm not waiting for just any brave man here in my loneliness, but for Odysseus. There are many strong brave men and even some of the Suitors were so, but there is only one Odysseus and I am waiting for him, my dear Eurycleia, even though his return is tied to the thinnest strand of hope. Until I have certain news of his having been swallowed by the ocean's waves or having perished in an ambush, I will wait for him, and I will not fall victim to any deception, not even to the naive and impassioned voice of my old nurse. I know you hate to see me alone, and I understand your kindhearted feelings, but I'm not looking for just any husband, otherwise I would have married one of the Suitors. I know that there is little chance of Odysseus returning, but I will hold on to that small chance, and I neither seek nor want any other remedy to my solitude."

I already knew Eurycleia would not give up.

"For years you have disparaged the Suitors inhabiting your house, devouring even the stones, but now you are saying things that are bitter to my ears. I have not come to you proposing a marriage to an unknown hero or a braggart. I announced that the guest Telemachus introduced into your house is Odysseus—this is the truth that you find a hundred ways to deny. My age and my experience have not tricked me, but when you find yourself next to him in front of the fireplace where he awaits, you yourself will recognize him, not merely from his appearance but from a gaze, his voice, a gesture, from all those subtle and mysterious clues of love. Unless the separation of all these years has made you deaf and blind and erased even the memory of the love that bound you to him once upon a time."

I stroked Eurycleia's white hair, but remained steadfast in my determination not to give in to her pleading.

"Your heartfelt words and the duties of hospitality have convinced me to go downstairs to the banquet hall, but before presenting myself before a foreign guest who has shown so much bravery and who is said to be of noble birth, I must put on a dress fit for a queen."

The old nurse Eurycleia combed my hair in silence and helped me knot it behind my neck with a golden clasp, and then she took my most beautiful linen tunic and a gold-fringed mantle from a chest. When I pulled the lapis lazuli necklace from a jewelry box, Eurycleia immediately tried to advise against it.

"Why, my dear Penelope, do you want to put this necklace on again, one that Odysseus cannot recognize? I wish you would throw it into the deep sea to avoid pointless suspicions from arising in your husband's heart. But if you want to keep it, I beg you not to show it off on a day like today."

"Our guest has already seen this necklace, but if I thought that he were truly Odysseus," I replied, "I would never have worn it again. But even you can see that the lapis lazuli color matches my sea-blue tunic and that the specks of gold sparkling in the stone go well with the golden fringe of the mantle. I do not have many opportunities to welcome foreign guests in my house, and so I would like to be dressed appropriately. Even in our pain and sadness, all women have a little room left for vanity."

Eurycleia walked away in silence without even helping me put on my clothes. So I called for Eurynome, the other silent nurse who came to the palace at the time of my wedding, and I had her help me put on the tunic and the mantle and to put the finishing touches on my hair.

ODYSSEUS

I decided to reveal myself to Penelope still wearing the beggar's rags that I had on my back when I first arrived at my house, and holding the bow of vengeance. Penelope came down the stairs solemnly and came near me, nodding her head slightly. What's this, I asked myself, didn't Eurycleia tell her anything? I can't understand this haughty attitude, this icy gaze as if the massacre of the Suitors had not freed her from a burden but had caused unexpected pain. She sat down at the fireplace in front of me without saying a word.

Telemachus came to my aid from the back of the hall, and he rebuked his mother sternly.

"Most sad mother with a callous heart, why aren't you embracing my father, who has returned to his homeland after so many years and who, at grave risk to himself, has freed our house from the plague of the Suitors? What is troubling your soul? Why won't you speak? Have you nothing to say to your husband? Why aren't you asking him any questions? He humbly chose to show himself to you in the clothes of a beggar, and now he poignantly begs for a smile from you, for a soft word of affection. But I see that not a single tear has fallen from your eyes, and not a single word has come from your lips."

"Out of a thousand men," Penelope said, "I would be able to recognize Odysseus even after a hundred years. But this stranger, be he a beggar or be he a scion of illustrious stock as he brags, is nothing but a simulacrum of Odysseus, a fiction, a falsehood that has furtively crept into our house. He has been an invaluable ally in your battle against the Suitors, and now you are in his dept with enormous gratitude, but you cannot offer him your mother as a reward, as if she were a commodity. Respect my feelings, Telemachus, and let me decide if this man is an impostor as I believe, or if the passing years have truly erased Odysseus' features from his face to such an extent that I can no longer recognize him. But if the war and the long voyage home have changed him so dramatically, then once again may that war be damned, and that voyage be damned."

Telemachus immediately rebelled against her words.

"If you don't recognize his features, does your heart tell you nothing?"

"Remember, Telemachus, that you were a tiny boy when your father left for the Trojan War, and so it was easy for you to fall into the trap laid by this stranger. But I was a woman, not a child, the day he left, and so leave it up to me to recognize him, and don't scold me unnecessarily."

My heart froze at Penelope's words. Penelope hasn't recognized me and she scolded Telemachus for wanting to put her up for sale. And I would be an impostor. Why do the gods persecute me, and why have they made me vanish from Penelope's heart? In one way, though, I should pay attention to her words and recognize their wisdom, when she damns the war and my overlong voyage home.

"My soul," I said to her, "I have dreamed of this day for twenty years. I thought about you under the walls of Troy when darkness fell on the Achaean army, and I always talked about you with my fellow warriors, and I kept a loving memory of you alive every time I left on a dangerous mission. My thoughts ran to you when storms made my ship shake under hostile waves. Or when ferocious Polyphemus took us prisoner in his cavern and deprived me of my best companions. And now that I have cleared the house of all the admirers, you look at me as if I were a stranger, and you invite me to leave my island and my house once again. I listened to your voice inside a smooth shell for years until a violent wave tore it from my hands during a shipwreck, but now, have I lost my wife along with that shell?"

And again, while I spoke these words, I could not hold back the untimely tears that began to roll down my cheeks.

"There's your proof that this beggar is not Odysseus," Penelope exclaimed, speaking to Telemachus. "Odysseus has a tough heart, and I have never seen a tear fall from his eyes, not even when he said goodbye to me before boarding the ship headed for Troy along with the other Achaeans. Tears do not become Odysseus, whom I never saw cry during the years of our marriage, not out of joy, and not out of sadness. A man who cries in front of a woman without feeling ashamed cannot be Odysseus. Let this man take his leave and face his destiny. You, Telemachus, will give him the tunic and woolen mantle that I promised, and the boots will soon be ready too. And you will see to it that he is compensated for the valorous assistance he gave to you in eliminating the usurpers and regaining your realm. Let the two of you agree upon a generous price. If, on the other hand, this foreigner wishes to take a rest here as our guest, let him be welcomed with open arms, and he shall have a seat at our table and a bed in our house."

I knew that these unexpected and untimely tears would end up ruining my reputation. Tears do not become Odysseus, Penelope said, and how can I blame her? I've been betrayed by this weakness that has tortured me since I stepped foot on my island. And thus it is, after massacring the Suitors, after all of the agonies and dangers of this undertaking, here I am, defeated by my own tears.

"Perhaps these beggar's clothes still stained with blood mar my appearance," I said to Penelope, "and thus I think it is time for me to put on the tunic and mantle that you generously promised me. The old nurse Eurycleia can wash and oil my limbs so as to make me seem worthy of the hospitality that you have offered. How could I sit at your table still wearing the rags under which I hid in order to trick those who had brutally taken over my house and my rights, but that, alas, have tricked my wife too?"

"I ordered the seamstresses to prepare dignified clothes for our guest," Penelope said to Telemachus, "but the seamstresses need more time to finish their work."

And again Telemachus spoke up.

"I ask you, Mother, to offer our guest, whom I have recognized as my father, the clothes of Odysseus that you keep in the upper rooms of the house in a large chest. If you don't recognize our guest as your husband, allow me to make this decision, of which I solemnly take all responsibility. My will is that our guest shall wear Odysseus' clothes, which have been jealously guarded as a memory and in the hopes of his return. I tell you that my father Odysseus has returned and that he can honorably wear his former clothes."

"I bow to your will," Penelope said, "even though it disgusts me to take out Odysseus' clothes just so this wanderer, by your naive designs, can look like the king of Ithaca. I personally shall go to open the chest with the key that I have jealously guarded for all these years, but it will take more than Odysseus' clothes to convince me of his vaunted identity. And in the meantime, may our guest get ready with the necessary washing and cleanse himself of blood before putting on the precious clothes of the king of Ithaca."

The old nurse Eurycleia led me to a corner of the great hall, had me sit on a stool, with experienced hands wiped my body with a soft sponge soaked in hot water scented with citronella, and finally oiled my entire body with pure olive oil, massaging my limbs until they were shiny and smooth.

The old woman didn't say a single word during the washing, nor did I want to question her. I entered my house like a stranger and now Penelope has made me even stranger, and while the real Odysseus was standing there in front of her eyes, she continued to chase after a shadow. I am that pathetic shadow, whose misadventures never seem to end. Without being recognized by Penelope, I was still that beggar I had pretended to be, the prisoner of my own masquerade. Into what state of nothingness had I fallen? Was I truly Nobody, as I had made Polyphemus believe? But I was not in the Cyclops' cave here; I was in my homeland, in my palace, in front of Penelope, who watched me through the eyes of a stranger.

At last, two handmaidens arrived carrying a white linen tunic and a crimson mantle with silver decorations. I had a hard time getting into the tunic, which was too tight in the shoulders and squeezed the rest of my body. I tried to hide the overly tight tunic under the crimson mantle and I presented myself shyly to

Penelope, whose stubbornness has managed to make me doubt even myself.

PENELOPE

I accepted Telemachus' idea, or should I say his order, to have Odysseus put on the tunic and mantle of Odysseus. I spied on him from the top of the stairs and I was amazed to see that his skin is not covered in scars as I imagined to be the case with all war veterans, and that instead, aside from the scar on his leg, it is all as smooth and solid as bronze.

When he came before us wearing that old tunic that squeezed his entire body, I chose not to make any comment, since everyone has eyes to see, but a despairing shiver ran through me. Who will ever be able to give me back all the years that the gods took away? Odysseus filled his days fighting and then seeking adventure in the wide world, but I waited for him closed up in my solitude as if in a prison, besieged by the horde of Suitors. I will never get back the lost time or the love that I kept alive only in my memories. But remembering is not living. Hoping and waiting is not living.

Odysseus is still handsome and strong, a bit less the hero finally with those overtight clothes on his back, that crumpled fringe, those slight stains of mildew on the whiteness of the fabric. But I ask myself again, now that he is in front of me, What happened to him after the end of the war? Odysseus was always an expert sailor and could not have been tricked by the sea. So why did he choose to run mortal risks in storms at sea, in Polyphemus' cave, and in the whirlpools between Scylla and Charybdis rather than turn his ship immediately toward Ithaca?

It almost seems as if Odysseus, the great storyteller and master of disguise, chased these many adventures just to be able to recount them. I have heard how he enchanted everyone with his stories in the palace of the Phaeacians, to such an extent that they didn't want to let him leave. This is the reason, it seems, that he stayed there for so long, and why they heaped gifts on him when he left. But someone told me about Nausicaa, the daughter of the king who hosted him, who fell in love with the illustrious hero who had arrived naked on their shores after a storm. But who can tell true from false anymore? Does the difference even matter?

Odysseus is vain, and I already know that after the defeat of the Suitors he will repeat the story of the massacre a thousand times here in this house and elsewhere, and every time, the story will be different depending on the day, on his imagination, on who is listening to him. No doubt when he disguised himself as a beggar in order to confront the Suitors with the bow and sword, he was already thinking about the magnificent story he would be able to make out of it during long winter evenings in front of the fireplace.

Let's face it, Odysseus doesn't just tell stories about what happens to him, he also makes things happen in order to tell stories about them. I'm sure that I myself will be the subject of his stories, even if my stubbornness will be a bitter memory for a long time. His life is a great factory of fictions, of lies, of secrets, of enigmas. But beyond the truth that he so often hides with his fictions and his disguises, there is something that Odysseus has never spoken about, not even with Telemachus, a secret that he is scrupulously keeping in some corner of this island, but which I have uncovered by the words that have slipped from his own imaginary stories. I wonder where he has hidden the expensive gifts received from the king of the Phaeacians. That gold and silver are not imaginary. But what is the reason for all this secrecy?

After all, it is not only his bravery that I have always admired but also his imagination, which embellishes and brightens everything. Maybe this is really the reason that I love him, his boundless ability to give free rein to his thoughts and imagination, to let them run like the wind.

We all know how to pretend, and a lie can often be convenient and honest, but I lie only out of necessity and not for the pleasure of it like Odysseus. When I heard that this wanderer, landed in Ithaca from who knows where, had been telling stories about his adventures from Crete to Troy to Egypt countless times in countless different versions, I immediately thought he might be Odysseus, even before seeing him. Men are no less vain and talkative than women, but who could have gone on and on recounting those preposterous adventures with all those ever-changing details? And the best part is that he himself always ends up believing his own stories.

Now Odysseus is in front of me, wearing those old clothes exhumed from a chest, that overly tight tunic that he tried to hide beneath the crimson mantle. Telemachus immediately noticed that Odysseus' old tunic no longer fit his shoulders, but he rightly gave little importance to this fact.

"In these many years," he said, "Odysseus' body has become more solid because of his struggles and his age, as happens to every man, and thus we should not be surprised if these clothes no longer fit him."

I've noticed that every time Telemachus speaks of his father he deliberately calls him Odysseus, perhaps out of respect or perhaps to emphasize his certainty to me, and in hopes of melting my reserve.

I chose not to reply to Telemachus' words because my voice would have betrayed the feelings that stuck in my throat upon seeing Odysseus dressed in his clothes from twenty years ago. For a moment I would have liked to give in to my emotions and run to him, hugging him and covering him with kisses, but I was able to hold myself back because I cannot forget even for a moment the affront that I have suffered. Odysseus deserves to be punished by the patient, generous, mild Penelope. Though it took him but one day to defeat all of my admirers, he'll have to fight much longer to reconquer the offended Penelope.

The situation had become practically unbearable to me. I didn't know where to look, what to say in order to break that terrible silence, how to hide the trembling of my hands. So I said that it was time to eat and that the kitchen servants were ready to bring the meal to the table.

Odysseus watched me, attempted to smile, to glean something from my eyes that was not there, because my heart, as Telemachus had rightly said, was truly becoming as hard as stone.

Odysseus stared fixedly at the lapis lazuli necklace that I was wearing around my neck without daring to ask me about it. He certainly knew that it had not been a part of my jewelry when he left. And so where did it come from? It was not hard to see that the necklace had unsettled him, seeing as how it could be a sign of adultery, but it was also a confirmation that I didn't believe that he was the real Odysseus—otherwise I never would have put it on such display.

During the meal, Odysseus was forced to retract his stories about his adventures in Egypt and all the stories told while disguised as the beggar, putting even Telemachus in a difficult position. Following my unrelenting refusal, perhaps even he was now beginning to harbor some doubts. If I showed so much tenacity and conviction in not recognizing Odysseus, how could he be certain that this was his father, he who could not remem-

ber him at all? Were some memories about the house, the trial of
the bow, and a scar enough to claim that this was really Odysseus? The world is a large place, and there are many strong men
who can bend a bow.

Poor Telemachus, the way I have acted must have created so
many doubts in his soul. I had hidden my joy at having Odysseus
by my side so well that the entire meal was filled with silences, and
Odysseus had to suffer through that disquieting atmosphere, over
which hung the suspicion of fakery and all of the blood that you
could still smell in the air despite the water and the sulfur fumes.

The sickly-sweet smell of human blood is disgusting. Not
even the sulfur was able to chase it away, or was it just my imagination? But even imagination can overtake our senses, and the
smell of blood, real or imagined, had made me lose my appetite,
and that of Odysseus and Telemachus as well, who barely
touched the abundant food that the kitchen servants had brought
to the long table.

ODYSSEUS

Before going to bed, we sat down in front of the fire, with ornate
cups full of wine for Telemachus and me, and limeflower tea for
Penelope. I can tell that Telemachus is worried. He stared at me
lengthily and then suddenly walked off to hang his lance and
sword, which the handmaidens had laid against a stool in a corner
of the great hall. But it was only a ruse, for he called to Eurycleia
and began whispering with her, no doubt to get some reassurance
about who I am. Or maybe he wanted to leave me alone with
Penelope, hoping that we would unravel the snarl of my identity.

With silent Penelope before me, I searched my memories for
any secret detail by which I could be recognized. Beneath the

walls of Troy, all of us spoke about our women, telling uninhibited stories that took wing in the dark solitude of our encamp-
ment. I spoke about Penelope, I described her body just as my
companions had described the bodies of their wives, the color
and length of her hair, her firm, sensitive breasts, the deep navel
that shaped her soft belly, and then the most secret places of her
body, hidden beneath a thick bush, and of a mole above one of
her knees that I would stare at when Penelope lay naked on the
bed. I now tried as hard as I could to remember if that mole
I told my companions about was above her right or left knee, but
the goddess Mnemosyne has betrayed me.

No matter how much I tried, I was unable to remember which
side that mole was on. If I had told Penelope about it, as a secret
that only Odysseus could know, I would have had half a chance
of guessing right and half a chance of making a fatal mistake. I
was close to taking my chances, but then I decided not to risk it.
Penelope has turned me into a coward.

A great emptiness, and interminable silence when Penelope
and I are alone. Do we have nothing to say to each other? But
when Telemachus came back and sat down near us, a new story
that could help my cause surfaced in my confused mind.

I had personally built our bed, using the trunk and branches
of an old olive tree that grew in our courtyard and that had
twined itself into the wall of our house at the time of Telemachus' birth, when we decided to build on extra rooms, including
a new bedroom for Penelope and me. With my hatchet and plane
I hewed and shaped the great olive tree's upper branches that
reached the top floor. And so the bed was supported by those
branches, which I then sculpted under the guidance of an expert
woodworker. I told all these details to Penelope, in Telemachus'

presence, and they should have served as proof that I knew even the most secret parts of this house.

"Your story is absolutely true," Penelope immediately admitted, "but this certainly does not prove that you are Odysseus. I know for a fact that Odysseus bragged to everyone about his work on our bed, and he must have spoken about it with his companions during the long nights of the siege, when the Achaeans put down their arms, awaiting another day. Have you not perhaps told us that you also listened to his tales? We know that Odysseus gathered his companions around a great fire and spoke about Ithaca, about the wild-boar hunts and the scars, about the gardens planted by his father Laertes, about the pig farms and the oak forests filled with acorns. Certainly, then, also about his house, the bed built with his own two hands, and Penelope. The scar that you offer me as proof of your identity is not only common amongst hunters, but I recall Odysseus having that thick mark on his right leg, even though Eurycleia believes that he was wounded on his left leg, just like our guest. I don't know whether my recollections or those of an aged nurse with a faulty memory are of greater value."

Truth vacillates and slips away like a wave, and Penelope stubbornly rejected my every memory and skillfully found arguments that threw my proofs into disarray. Who knows if she truly believed what she was saying.

"I'll tell you a story, then," Penelope said, "that I doubt Odysseus ever told his companions, and which you thus cannot know."

"All men have something to hide."

"Odysseus, like Achilles and other warriors who would go on to fight heroically, tried everything to avoid leaving," continued

Penelope. "When the chiefs of the Achaeans came through Ithaca on their way to the Trojan shores, Odysseus threw a dunce's cap on his head, yoked an ox and donkey together, and began to plow the sand of the beach, seeding the furrows with handfuls of sand. But to no use, because a certain Palamedes, general of the Achaeans, took the baby Telemachus from his crib and placed him in front of the plowshare. And Odysseus halted the animals immediately, proving that he was perfectly sane. And so he too had to take up arms and leave for the war along with the others."

Telemachus looked at me, in disbelief and dismay.

"What you say truly happened, but I have chosen to forget it."

"Everyone on Ithaca knows the story," said Penelope, "but Odysseus certainly never told it to his companions, and thus you couldn't have heard it. This is why you didn't use it as proof that you are Odysseus."

"Memory makes its choices, and the real Odysseus, who you have here in front of you, didn't want to remember an episode from his life that he is still ashamed of. It is my shame that is my proof, just as it is proof that I would have preferred to stay in Ithaca with Penelope and Telemachus instead of going to the Trojan War."

"You find a rationale for everything," Penelope said sharply, "but I can see that this episode has surprised and embarrassed you. The real Odysseus would not have been surprised, since it happened to him, nor embarrassed, since he was aware that I already knew about it."

Pride and shame have thus betrayed me, and once again Penelope has shown herself to be even more cunning than the cunning Odysseus.

A deathly silence followed Penelope's words, and Telemachus was staring at the floor crestfallen and embittered, when the herald Medon came into the great hall to announce a new, unexpected danger.

"Word is spreading throughout town that the relatives and friends of the princes you have killed are arming themselves and have decided to take revenge for their deaths."

"New ambushes are thus being prepared against us," Telemachus said, "and we must prepare for new battles in order to defend ourselves. We overcame the first and most terrible calamity by shedding much blood, but we can't go on with such slaughters, we can't kill half of everybody."

And so I intervened, saying that we needed to call the singer Terpiade to us immediately, the one whose life we had spared, and organize a feast in the palace for the return of Odysseus, with great clamor and songs, so that everyone in town would be pleased, but also fearful and discouraged from trying any retaliation.

My proposal was immediately approved by Telemachus, but Penelope cooled our enthusiasm.

"I will accept this fiction of Odysseus' return," she said, "so that the friends and relatives of the killed princes will not rebel and will accept the massacre they brought upon themselves by their wicked ways. But don't think that this fiction, which for me represents yet another torment, will convince me to believe that Odysseus is this beggar whom we have welcomed into our house, not until my heart is convinced of it."

"That's not the reason for this feast," I said frankly to Penelope.

And so that night a strange scene was played out, wretched for me, even more miserable than for Penelope, while Terpiade was called to sing at the top of his lungs so that his voice could be heard from the streets.

A stiff wind had come up over the island, whistling through the windows and beneath the doors, dragging with it into the streets of Ithaca the songs and sounds of our feast, as well as the dust of the dry season.

"I know this wind that comes from the black continent well. It is called Eurus, and is as loved by sailors as it is hated by farmers, because it dries the soil and damages the crops."

"I see you are well versed in the winds from the sea as well as the land, like all travelers," Penelope said.

At this, I moved off toward one of the most beautiful of the handmaidens, slipped my arm around her waist, pulled her close to me while Penelope was watching, and spun her around the great hall to the tune of the cithara that accompanied Terpiade's strong, harmonious voice. And after the dance, while the singer still sang out loudly as he had been ordered to do, I came close to Penelope.

"Miserable and cruel among women," I said to her, "the gods have made your heart hard and now you refuse to recognize the man who sailed the tempestuous seas and ran risks of every nature to come back to his conjugal home. I will tell the nurse to prepare a separate bed, and I will not ask you to open your arms to me in the bed that I made with my own two hands. I will ask nothing of your heart of stone because I know I will receive nothing, and I don't even know if I want anything anymore. May our destinies remain separate. I will wait only until the sturdy boots that you ordered for me have been made, then I can finally return to my voyage along the roads of the world, now that I have freed Telemachus from the horde of usurpers."

As I pronounced these words, there they were again, those tears that filled my eyes and forced me to turn my face so that they would not be seen by Penelope, who had already upbraided me for this weakness before. Even the hands that had firmly bent my bow and grasped my sword now shook like those of an old man whose strength has been depleted by the years and the furies of fate.

"I see you turn your back on me after I have taken you in and generously offered my hospitality and promised you gifts that you will receive from my own hands," Penelope said at this point. "I've never met such an arrogant vagrant amongst all the vagrants who try to find food and shelter in my house. Don't think that this rudeness of yours makes you contemptible in my eyes, though, because in spite of my abhorrence of blood, I have always admired courage above all things. You have shown yourself courageous enough, and I would not want to call into question something so obvious that even a blind man could see it. But I do not recognize you as Odysseus, and thus you will not enter my bed even if you claim to have built it with your own hands. That you are a master of lies and trickery we have all seen more than once since your arrival on this island, but your lying tales are like the fables told at night around the fire, an innocent pastime, while your desire to identify yourself with Odysseus has the same dishonest motives as the Suitors, that you want to possess Odysseus' woman and his wealth, which now belongs to Telemachus as his legitimate heir. He owes you much, yes, but I repeat, not so much as to offer his mother as payment. Handmaidens, prepare a proper bed for our guest and let's wish him goodnight, for the day was hard and bloody for him."

These were the words with which Penelope ushered me into another night of restless sleep.

PENELOPE

The astute, the ingenious, the lying, the cocky, the fearsome Odysseus was as lost and fretful as a little bird stuck in birdlime, his hands shaking and his eyes brimming with shameful tears that he tried vainly to hide. I could barely hold my will against this pathetic scene. While the handmaidens prepared his bed for the night, Odysseus remained seated close to me in front of the burning fire.

"I see that you always change your reasons for denying my evidence," he said with extreme humility, "and you have not even believed the most intimate secrets from our marriage, like the story about the bed that I built with my hands, and even more so with my heart, from the branches of an old olive tree. Now, let me ask you a question about this lapis lazuli necklace that you are wearing around your neck and that you did not own when I left for the Trojan War. Tell me, Penelope, how I can claim with utter certainty that this necklace was never around your neck in those far-off years when no clouds darkened our marriage? I don't want to know who gave you this gift, because if you will not accept me as Odysseus I have lost every right to know. But in the name of the gods, how can a wandering stranger affirm that this necklace was not a gift from Odysseus, but from someone more recently?"

Odysseus had put me in a tight spot and now I had to quickly throw up an answer to his question and his clever doubts. I bowed my head and caressed the shining stones of the necklace with my fingers before replying.

"You, stranger, think that Antinous or another of my admirers gave me this necklace as collateral for a future wedding, but it is not so. You know that a desperate and lonely woman does not lose the pleasure of embellishing her person. This is no crime, just a feminine weakness that all men should understand. One day, a Phoenician merchant with dusty feet came through here, carrying a case of his goods. Amongst them—ivory combs, ribbons of silk and crimson, clasps and brooches of bronze and gold, amber bracelets and necklaces—there was this lapis lazuli necklace, which I admired for its excellent workmanship, for the quality of its stones flecked with so many golden specks, and for the precious gold-engraved catch. The price was reasonable, and I decided that I could allow myself this small pleasure in order to lessen my suffering and distract myself from the daily offenses of the Suitors and from the destruction of our herds. I paid the seven gold coins that the merchant wanted and I kept the necklace in a chest for the happy day when I would wear it to celebrate the return of Odysseus to his home of Ithaca. Because I still then believed in his return. Now that this hope has vanished, I thought that the return of Telemachus and the victory over the Suitors deserved my most elegant garments and this precious ornament that you have noticed around my neck. I hope, therefore, that your poisonous thoughts have received a satisfying answer, even if I am truly not bound to give any explanations about my life to a stranger. I will admit that you know much about Odysseus, but when men start speaking about their women, their tongues know no limits. No surprise, then, that you have learned many secrets from Odysseus' mouth. If your curiosity is still tormenting your soul, I could tell you about my sleepless nights spent questioning the stars, the interminable passing of the seasons, the agonizing solitude and boredom of so many futile springs, and the weeping that has worn out my eyes. Should I tell you about how I can no longer look at the lights in the starry sky without getting them confused? What can all of this add to your curiosity, or to my public image as a woman wounded by fate?"

ODYSSEUS

A strange and sad speech has Penelope dedicated to me. Why on earth would she respond to my challenge with an intimate story so heartbreaking as to almost suggest she were asking for compassion and respect? And why, when speaking about the voracious Suitors, did she say our herds and not my herds? Why ours? Her words disoriented me, and the suspicious provenance of that necklace provoked such a pathetic confession of her weakness that I was shaken and upset, even if I had not gotten an answer to my question. And why did she say that she would have worn that necklace only on the day of Odysseus' return to Ithaca? Why then did she put it on to meet me for the first time, even though she was certain I am not Odysseus?

As much as she insists on seeing me as a stranger, Penelope's heartfelt words deserved a reply that in some manner matched her own confession.

"This void of time has been endless for you, but for me as well, my adored Penelope, and so I tried to fill it with worthy deeds, but also with inexcusable errors. If I review the years passed in my travels, I see many dangers avoided, many adventures forced on me by fate, but also many useless risks that weigh on my conscience because they brought about the ruin of my faithful travel companions and delayed my return. Now I no longer think about the past, and you too, Penelope, forget the herds devoured by the Suitors, because this is not the time for memory. Now, together with Telemachus, I have carried out the vengeance that we decided upon together, and I therefore beg you to give me back my rags and my wanderer's satchel, because from your cruelty I want no payment. Along with my ragged clothes I will accept from you as a gift only those boots that you promised for my departure, because

I will not remain close to those who do not recognize me, not even if I were showered with crimson and gold. For a full ten years I sailed the seas and often landed in inhospitable lands. I will begin my voyage anew toward unknown shores where perhaps I will discover the affection, or love, that I have not found here in my house. My adored Penelope, let me find the boots that you promised near my bed tomorrow morning so that I can take up my wandering. Hard and merciless is your heart, Penelope, and I will flee from you like I fled from the Scylla and Charybdis."

"Why compare me to two sea monsters, you ungrateful guest? If you were truly Odysseus, you should perhaps compare me to the perfidious Calypso. And why not to the tender and hateful Nausicaa?"

"What are you trying to say? Open your thoughts to a confused and desperate man."

But Penelope righted herself immediately.

"By now, I can accept anything that happens to me—I even accepted these new unsettling events that have been heaped upon the ancient ones. And I envy your madness, stranger, that lets you sail through a world of your own imagination."

Rather than answer me, Penelope simply repeated her promise, her sad promise, that the following morning I would find the new boots together with my satchel and beggar's clothes next to my bed.

"Encourage Telemachus," I told her again, "to defend his house, his land, and his mother Penelope, together with the loyal men who remained at his side in his gravest moments and who will be of assistance to him again. You will embrace him for me and tell him that I cannot stay in my homeland if the person for whom I returned persists in not recognizing me. Repeat my words, I beg you, so that he does not think that I have abandoned him for an unhealthy desire for adventure. When I leave this house, I will go to embrace my elderly father Laertes, who lives in the countryside, unaware of all that has happened, and from there I will head to the coast and wait for passage on a merchant ship, and sail with the crew wherever their trade takes them. It will be a voyage with no purpose, and my only destination shall be time itself, which pitilessly eats away at all men."

PENELOPE

I listened to Odysseus' fervent speech with indescribable pity, but I had to continue to pretend not to recognize him; I had to make him pay, at any price, for his slighting of me. He has taught me well how to carry out an intrigue, even if it exhausts and pains me.

I have no one I can confide my secret to, and I will spend another night speaking to the stars. Odysseus says the world is almost limitless. What does he mean? Is he mad? Or am I the one who is mad with my underhanded revenge?

ODYSSEUS

Who knows, maybe Penelope is acting out her own perverse play to get revenge not so much for my adventures during my voyage home as for having kept her in the dark about my true identity before the massacre. She keeps stubbornly denying it, but I think she has recognized me as Odysseus. She was indeed too upset when I told her that I would wait on the shore for a passing ship to put me back at sea. I even think she put that lapis lazuli necklace on to make me jealous.

A purchase from a Phoenician merchant is not unrealistic, if I didn't know that she too is capable of lying. It will be easy for me to verify Penelope's story by questioning loyal Eurycleia, who undoubtedly was present during the purchase, if purchase there was. Unfortunately, Eurycleia is also loyal to Penelope; and then, she is a woman, expert in lying like all women. Will I ever learn the truth, supposing that only one truth even exists under the sky?

I do think, though, that Penelope will have a worse night than me, and that she will try to console herself by questioning the stars in the firmament through—as she describes it, hoping to soften me—misty eyes.

PENELOPE

I've pushed things to the breaking point, but I had no other choice. The excitement of having Odysseus in front of me has been snuffed out by my despicable thirst for revenge. Will the gods forgive me for this unworthy feeling, which has replaced twenty years lived slowly and painfully?

And here I am again, suffering dreadful agonies and creating no less dreadful agonies for Odysseus. I have never been one for suffering, but events have forced me into this cruel behavior in which I honestly can barely recognize myself.

Odysseus is confused, but how could it be otherwise? I understand that he wanted to take revenge and that Telemachus hoped to win his realm back, but seeing Odysseus in the role of the ferocious avenger somehow turned him into a stranger for me. How can I lie down in the same bed with him after all the blood spattered in fury, with a strange kind of pleasure, here in our house? The corpses of the young Suitors skewered by his sword and dripping blood, their eyes staring into nothingness, are frightening images that chase after me day and night. Whatever his reasons, a man who kills another man is a monster to me. But what am I saying? Is the world then populated by monsters? Is Odysseus a monster too? Unfortunately, even the gods themselves are violent and bloody, and it is they who justify the violence of men.

I don't understand on what pretext Odysseus has doubted my faithfulness. Did he not perhaps repeatedly betray me during his voyages? Is it perhaps less painful for a woman to be betrayed by her man than a man to be betrayed by his woman? Who decreed that a woman should suffer and forgive? I will forgive him, but this forgiveness will never make up for my suffering, grown as high as the highest mountain in Ithaca.

I will not have him find those new boots next to his bed tomorrow. I tricked the Suitors for years weaving and unraveling the shroud, so shouldn't I be able to endlessly delay Odysseus' departure by leaving him barefoot? But his arrogance went too far when he questioned Eurycleia about the origins of that necklace. Does he really think I sold myself for those lapis lazuli stones? Is this what Odysseus thinks of me? Eurycleia, who feels guilty for not having immediately told me about Odysseus' arrival, repeated the story about the Phoenician merchant as I had ordered her to do. She obeys orders, whether they come from me or from Odysseus. She is a wise woman who can adapt to a two-sided loyalty.

I would never be able to explain the truth to the suspicious Odysseus, and thus I decided that an honest lie was in my best interests. I really do feel some remorse about having accepted the necklace from Ctesippus, but it was only given as partial compensation, not as a gift, and in truth, fat Ctesippus never expected anything in return. If the thought that Penelope has given her favors for a necklace has passed through Odysseus' mind, it is a new and devastating insult that spurs me even further toward revenge. Patient, kind, sweet Penelope was not willing to tolerate the Suitors' indecency yesterday, and she is not willing to bear the fact that Odysseus has such squalid thoughts about her today.

I have reluctantly thrown a phial of Asian perfume into the sea, a gift from I don't remember whom, in order to avoid raising other doubts in Odysseus' mind after the necklace.

I've become practiced in lying and dissembling, but I was not able to control my emotions when Odysseus declared himself ready to take up his wandering again. I believe he was sincerely upset, but he won't be able to choose to leave tomorrow morning, because he won't find the boots I promised him. A promise that hangs over me like a threat. Once upon a time, Odysseus confessed to me that his life's greatest desire was to satisfy his curiosity about the world, and that confession was a threat too.

In any event, I'm sure he's going to have a worse night than me.

ODYSSEUS

It is dawn, the most favorable moment for me to distance myself from the house while everyone is still enveloped in sleep. I'm leaving with my old, worn-out sandals on my feet and my satchel on my shoulder. I will have old Laertes recognize me, in part to humiliate the mistrustful Penelope, and then I will decide what to do with my life.

The world is practically infinite, and I am an excellent sailor.

PENELOPE

Odysseus wasn't in his bed this morning. His ragged mantle and worn-out sandals are missing too. I struggled to stay on my feet, my knees shaking, and I couldn't breathe. I ran to old Eurycleia, who knew nothing about our guest and was surprised to learn that he had left. Then she reproached me again for having refused to recognize him as Odysseus in spite of all the evidence.

"I beseech you, Eurycleia, this is not the moment for reproaches."

I could not hold back the tears, and the old woman tried to console me and promised that she would send Telemachus to look for him on the roads of Ithaca.

"But why are you so upset," she said once again, maliciously, "if you're sure that he isn't Odysseus?"

I begged her not to humiliate me and to send Telemachus immediately in search of Odysseus. I then returned to my room and began to cry like I never had before in my life.

ODYSSEUS

Telemachus caught up with me while I was asking passersby on the roads of Ithaca for a piece of bread to put in my satchel, my feet wrapped in my old sandals and my beggar's rags on my back. He took me by the arm and begged me to come back home, because Penelope was tearing her hair out in desperation over my departure.

"And what will the citizens of Ithaca say if they see you begging in the streets? They are waiting to see and celebrate their king, not a beggar."

"In Penelope's eyes, I am a beggar."

"Crying, she begged me to bring you back to her. Isn't that compensation enough for your pride?"

I replied that Penelope could wait. The most important thing now was to see my elderly father Laertes in his house at the outskirts of the city.

"I want to embrace him, but I also want to be recognized," I told Telemachus, "since I am just an impostor to Penelope. The Suitors' villainy and abuses have been avenged with blood, but Penelope's insult deserves only my running away and returning to my wandering ways. After seeing Laertes, I will board the first ship that passes Ithaca, even if it should be a pirate ship. No one will be able to hold me back."

Telemachus became uneasy upon hearing that I was ready to leave again, but he didn't oppose my decision with the fervor that I expected. It's almost as if he has withdrawn into himself now that the Suitors have been eliminated, and that he has forgotten the joy of having found his father.

I already had the feeling this was the case, but now I am certain that Penelope's stubbornness in not wanting to recognize me was nothing more than a ruse to punish me for I know not what mistakes. Telemachus confirmed this by telling me about her desperation upon discovering that I had left. In truth, it was more a getaway than a departure.

If she wanted to humiliate me because I didn't tell her about my plans for revenge against the Suitors, she has been so successful that now I am the offended one, and I have truly decided to board the first ship that passes Ithaca. In the end, it won't be a great sacrifice, since my nature is that of an adventurer, a wanderer, an explorer of distant lands and people, carried along by winds and friendly fortune. And I can finally cast off these beggar's clothes and put an end to this pretending. Hidden under the branches of that wild olive tree on the beach, there is still the treasure that the king of the Phaeacians gave to me, and with that I will be able to purchase a small ship and hire a crew of expert sailors. There is a shipyard in Zakynthos where they make excellent ships with resinous cedarwood, and they say that they are quick with their work.

I asked Telemachus if it was best to immediately reveal myself to my elderly father Laertes, or if he thought I should present myself incognito in order for him to recognize me himself.

"Your old father can't readily take the strain of unexpected emotions, and thus it would be better if you didn't reveal yourself immediately, so that he himself can recognize you."

Telemachus' answer made me think that Penelope's suspicions have rubbed off on him, that not even he is certain of my identity anymore, and that he is waiting to see whether old Laertes will recognize me.

PENELOPE

Odysseus' unexpected departure has insinuated a terrible suspicion in my soul. How can it be possible that the real Odysseus renounces his wife and his house now that it has been emptied of the horde of admirers? Only a stranger could make such a decision that will bring him back to wandering the seas and unknown lands. Could my reluctance to identify him as Odysseus, spurred by ideas of revenge, have been born of a deeper understanding that I don't dare confess, not even to myself?

The only certain thing is my desperation, because be he the real Odysseus or not, I have recognized him as such, and that's what matters to me. I know that truth and fiction intertwine and become confused, but at this moment, the only man I can welcome into my bed as Odysseus is here in Ithaca. So long as he hasn't already boarded a passing ship.

My stubbornness has brought about the danger of a new, tragic solitude that I am not ready for. The voracious Suitors were preferable to solitude. Am I just raving? I have thrown open the doors to my own ruin, depriving myself of this man, who out of pride is now willing to abandon everything and take up his vagabond life anew. Or does he know exactly where he is going, and does perhaps another woman wait for him there?

ODYSSEUS

I found old Laertes in the garden with a hoe in his hand, working the ground around the trunk of a young fruit tree. He was wearing a dirty tunic full of patches, while around his legs he had wrapped some sewn skins to protect them from the thorny brambles, and he wore gloves on his hands like a vegetable farmer. He had a goatskin cap that covered his forehead and was pulled down over his ears.

The former king of Ithaca truly looked no better than a wretched farmer, and I felt great pity for him. For a second I thought I would embrace him and tell him immediately that I was his son Odysseus, but I have to keep the promise I have already made to Telemachus.

"Your garden is well tended," I said to old Laertes, "and I see that you are expertly hoeing the ground around the roots of this tree so that it will bear good fruit. But your own appearance is unkempt, and your clothes are like those of a bum, like mine, and so I find it hard to believe that you are King Laertes, as I was told by young Telemachus. I landed on this island, which I have been told is Ithaca, in hopes of finding an old companion I met under the walls of Troy whom I have not seen since we took our leave at the end of the war, each returning to his native land. When I returned to Crete, my homeland, I discovered my house, my lands, and my herds in the hands of wicked usurpers, and I barely managed to escape their ambushes and continue my voyages. I am the lord of Alybas, son of Apheidas, of whom you may have heard, and my name is Eperitos. Now I wander the world begging for bread. I fear that you too have fallen slave to cruel usurpers, and that now you work like a slave on the lands that they have taken from you. I had promised Odysseus, which was the name of the companion I met under the walls of Troy, that I would have given him expensive presents if he visited my house in Crete. But if he ever managed to make it down there to my unhappy homeland, I don't know what kind of welcome he will have received from its new rulers."

Old Laertes raised his goatskin cap and looked at me through eyes that had suddenly brightened from emotion.

"This is indeed Ithaca, unlucky land fallen into the hands of violent men who keep Penelope, Odysseus' wife, prisoner in her own house. But tell me if you have any news about my son Odysseus since he left Troy, and if I can still hope that one day he too will land here in Ithaca, or if I must weep because he has fallen victim to the cruel ocean or to wild beasts in foreign lands."

"Five years have passed," I replied, "since Odysseus landed on the island of Trinacria and his men offended Apollo by killing the oxen of the sacred Herd of the Sun. I heard about this from some fishermen when my own ship was blown to those coasts by a squall. But the most recent news about Odysseus comes from the island of the Phaeacians, from which it seems he has already set sail for Ithaca."

At these words old Laertes was struck stock-still, and not a word fell from his lips, only tears from his eyes. And then I could no longer resist, and I embraced my elderly father, squeezing him tightly.

"It's me, your son Odysseus whom you have longed for, come home twenty years after his departure for the war in Troy. And now, my dear father, dry your tears, for the vile admirers who had set up camp in our palace have now tumbled into Hades' shades. Telemachus and I have killed them, with the help of two of our herdsmen.

Old Laertes turned his gaze upon Telemachus, then looked at me in wonder.

"How can I believe you? How can you have killed them? I know that there were a great number of Suitors, all of them young and armed."

And I promptly answered.

"The Suitors are no more—Telemachus can vouch for that—but we must still fear revenge from their relatives and friends."

"I can barely believe your words. Have the gods thus brought me such unexpected joy after making me suffer for so long? Show me, I beg of you, an irrefutable sign by which I can recognize you as my beloved son Odysseus. My eyes have grown old and I can't trust them anymore but, I beg you, show me a true sign or tell me some detail that only you and I can know."

So I uncovered my leg with the scar.

"You will recall, my dear father, the deep wound that the tusks of a wild boar left on me during a hunt on Mount Helicon. But if this is not enough, I can also tell you how just before my departure for Troy, we planted ten apple trees and forty fig trees together, so as to be able to dry the fruit in the oven and stock up for the winter."

"They were forty apples trees and ten figs, in truth. But numbers can easily be confused after many years. I therefore recognize you as my dear son Odysseus from these signs."

And saying thus, old Laertes embraced me and covered me in kisses. He then ordered his servants to prepare a rich banquet with plenty of wine to celebrate the return of his son. But

Telemachus remained quiet, and didn't share in the old man's joys.

"Though he may be old," he told me, "the father did not recognize his son, the same way the wife did not recognize her husband. Alas, how much damage has been done by distance and the passing of time."

I could hear from his voice that a poisonous suspicion had insinuated itself in Telemachus. Why had he suggested that I not reveal myself immediately to old Laertes? To see whether he recognized me, certainly. And then he didn't recognize me. Then I showed the scar, which Penelope has already rejected as proof, and I told the story of the fruit trees that we had planted together before my departure, but I mixed up the numbers. Odysseus could even have told the story about the fruit trees to his companions during the long windy nights under the walls of Troy. Penelope's suspicions have now infected Telemachus too. What use were the hugs and the tears of old Laertes and my imperfect memories if first Penelope and now Telemachus do not recognize me as Odysseus? What other realities have been concealed by my presence in this Ithaca of endless tears?

Halfway through the banquet we heard angry voices coming from the road, and we quickly grabbed our weapons, and old Laertes himself took up a sharp sword.

The herald Medon and the singer Terpiade were trying to calm a small crowd of armed men in the road who had come to hunt down Telemachus in revenge for the Suitors' deaths. But the weapons that we showed to the insurgents were more eloquent than the words of my two faithful subjects.

I threw my beggar's rags to the ground and spoke in a confident voice.

"We were able to defeat the brave young Suitors and we will just as easily make you fall bloodily. Other armed servants are inside the house and will come to our aid if you insist on using your weapons."

The rebels spoke among themselves softly without daring to approach. So I said other things to convince them to choose peace.

"We will not ask you to pay us back for the animals that were slaughtered for the banquets, and we will allow you to gather your dead so as to do as you wish with them or give them an honorable burial. But a single warlike gesture from you will let loose our rage, and more blood will seep into the arid ground of Ithaca. So think carefully. Take care of your dead, make crowns of myrtle for them if you want to accompany them on their final voyage, and then return to your homes in silence. And let it be known that from now on it shall not be me, Odysseus, who will rule Ithaca. Your lord will be my young son Telemachus, to whom I relinquish the throne and command of the island in a gesture of peace."

These words seemed to calm the souls of the rebels, who walked away from Laertes' house in silence.

Telemachus came to my side to ask if I really meant to renounce the rule of Ithaca, or if it was just a ruse to placate the rebel souls.

"The moment I decided not to stay on this island or in the house where I am rejected by my wife, you became the new king, for Ithaca cannot remain without a ruler."

"But Penelope is in despair over your departure. You can't cause her more pain."

"In despair over the departure of a vagabond for whom she ordered a pair of boots so he could clear out as quickly as possible? We freed her from the presence of the Suitors at great risk to our own lives, but I'm not sure if Penelope, deep down in her soul, is really happy about this liberation. You have every reason to be satisfied about it, but Penelope? As you recall, you too agreed to keep our plan a secret from her out of fear that she might speak to Antinous or Eurymachus or some other Suitor about it."

"I beg you," Telemachus then said, "return to the palace where Penelope is waiting for you in tears, I beg you, my dear father Odysseus."

What naive cunning to call me father Odysseus. Despite his doubts, then, Telemachus was willing to accept me as his father in his home just to save Penelope from sorrow.

We left Laertes, still holding his weapon, in the company of his servants at the house at the gates of the city, and we walked back to the palace in silence.

PENELOPE

Telemachus came to my room to tell me that Odysseus has returned. Then he told me that old Laertes had not recognized him, and that now even he fears that this is an impostor who heard Odysseus' secrets under the walls of Troy and has made use of them to get himself accepted as the king of Ithaca. Poor Telemachus, in the space of a few days you found your father and lost him again.

All of a sudden the roles have been reversed. I recognized Odysseus but pretended not to, and Telemachus, who welcomed him as his father Odysseus, now tries to insinuate even in me the suspicion that he is an impostor. My falsehood thus runs the risk of coinciding with an alternative possible truth, and my mind is confused. It is true that Laertes did not recognize him, but this proves nothing to me, for his mind has been wavering like an old ship on the waves of the sea for some time now.

I will thus go downstairs and embrace Odysseus, to whom I have always granted my love and my desperate admiration, along with my resentment of these past days. I am tired now, and want only a bit of peace.

Cleverly, Odysseus has relinquished the throne to Telemachus, and this could foment some new, reasonable suspicions. But why doesn't anyone care about my peace of mind? Why does Telemachus insinuate such terrible suspicions in my soul? It would be better if he started worrying about the problems of Ithaca, which are many. Hasn't Telemachus noticed the state of ruin our island is in? The rutted roads, the fields dried by wind, the decimated farms, the insufficient reservoirs. He needs to take care of these things if he hopes to obtain his subjects' approval.

I put my face back together after so many tears, I painted my cheeks and lips quickly, I combed my hair with the help of a handmaiden, and I put on my most beautiful clothes and the lapis lazuli necklace to show Odysseus one more time that it comes from innocent origins and that I have nothing to hide. Then I went downstairs into the great hall where Odysseus was waiting for me.

I ran to him and hugged him without being able to hold back my tears, tears of love and of joy this time. We embraced for a long time in silence under the watchful eyes of Telemachus, who chose not to join in our display of joy.

When we finally looked each other in the face, emotional and confused, Odysseus spoke to me with anxious words, which confirmed what I had already perceived and that no one could deny any longer. The truths of the world are many, but the only one that matters is the one that you have chosen according to the dictates of love and benevolent spirits.

"The seer Tiresias once told me that I would return to my homeland of Ithaca, but that I would leave again on another voyage to the lands beyond the sun, that a terrible storm would destroy my ship, and that I would perish in the deep sea along with my sailors."

Who knows if Tiresias' foreboding prediction had already been proven wrong by Odysseus' false departure, or if it referred to sometime in the future? Odysseus understood my concern and stroked my hair to console me.

"One other time," he said sincerely, "the gods had decreed my death and decided to have me perish in the tempestuous sea, but my stubborn willfulness reversed my fortunes. Now I will stay in Ithaca forever with my wife, until the day she gives me the boots that she ordered from an expert cobbler, but I hope that her love will delay their production, the same way the shroud was woven and unraveled to keep the Suitors' demands at bay."

I didn't need this pretext to keep Odysseus close to me, but I appreciated his idea for belying the prediction of Tiresias, augur of misfortune. My only path to recovery is by having the man whom I desire at my side during the day and in my marriage bed at night. After that, what do I care if anyone has doubts about him being the real Odysseus? I identified him as Odysseus from the very start, from his voice and his eyes, from his ambiguous smile and a hundred other little clues that are more reliable to me than the scar that convinced old Eurycleia. My instincts say that Odysseus has come home, and I don't want to hear any more about it, because this will save me from succumbing to the risk of a second terrible solitude.

Telemachus will rule the island as decreed by Odysseus, who will guide him with his advice, and this seems a wise decision that will allow me, after so many challenges, to finally start living my life again with the man who has been sent to me, or returned to me, by a merciful god.

ODYSSEUS

I have told so many lies that even I cannot free myself anymore from the tangled web that I wove with words about my persona. I didn't even resist the temptation to lie to myself, and I got so emotional that I cried every time I told those false, unhappy stories. Poets sing the endeavors of heroes, but I am not a poet, and I doubt I am a hero, even if I accomplished feats that others call memorable but that will vanish into the void of forgetting like the feats of all men who cannot find a poet to recount them.

Where are the poets? There were no poets under the walls of Troy and not even on the ships I sailed through the seas. If a man has fought even a single day he can tell a thousand war stories. If he has loved just a single woman he can tell a thousand love stories. But those who have not lived in love and in pain cannot invent anything aside from empty, arid words, like ash.

True heroes die young, either in battle or at the hand of traitors who envy their virtues. I am alive and must think about my life with Penelope, about winning back not only her love but her trust, about resting my soul and enjoying the fruits of my long hardship. I won't speak another word about that lapis lazuli necklace, even though I don't buy that story about the Phoenician merchant, no matter what Eurycleia says. It's implausible to find a traveling merchant carrying such precious, highly refined objects for sale. But even if Penelope lied to me and received it as a gift from Antinous, I'm certain she gave him nothing in return. Even though loneliness gives terrible advice, if Penelope had decided to give herself to one of the Suitors, be it Antinous or another, she would have done so by the light of day, thus eliminating all of the other admirers who crowded her house and devoured her herds.

I'm sure that one day or another that necklace, no matter how valuable, will get lost and never be found again.

More than once has Penelope complained to Telemachus and old Eurycleia about the animals that disappeared down the voracious gullets of her admirers. Wouldn't that also have been a legitimate reason, for a parsimonious woman like her, for putting an end to the slaughter if she had had any real feelings for one of them?

When she came down to the great hall, Penelope embraced me with such rapture that in a single moment she eradicated all of the mistrust that had changed our feelings ever since I stepped foot in the palace. She couldn't even speak from the emotion. She covered me with kisses and flooded me with tears that mixed with my own.

I wanted to say something in order to stop this rain of tears once again, so I suggested that she should make the preparation of my boots last as long as the weaving of the shroud, to keep Tiresias' prediction from coming true. It was like a defensive spell for our love, a joke to ward off any future departures.

I thought I saw that look of uncertainty on Telemachus' face again, but he was reassured after I repeated my decision to leave the rule of the island to him. He begged me to help him with my advice, and I appreciated this sign of humility and trust, even though I know that deep down in his soul he has his doubts about my being Odysseus. He wanted a father, and in the end he decided to welcome me as one. This is his truth.

I will certainly take a concern in my Ithaca again. I will have a small fleet built, not for warfare, but for trade. Our sailors will travel through the sea of the Peloponnesus and carry their goods to the most distant islands. And so I leave the tasks of the land to Telemachus, and I will handle the sea.

Eurycleia has taken up the rule of the house, and with the help of the handmaidens and the servants is tidying and cleaning the kitchens and storerooms; she has stocked up on oil, brine olives, and spices; she washed the black millstones for wheat and the coffer where honey and nuts are kept, then she washed the vases with seawater and fumigated them with sulfur for next year's wine.

Telemachus took a dozen workers with him to restore the palaestra and ordered the roads cleaned, the weeds pulled, and where necessary, the stones and drains refitted. Everyone is working enthusiastically and happily and praying to the gods for a rainfall from the sky that will cool the earth. Kids are tying belts around their waists and going into the woods, banging copper plates to hunt for wild bee swarms that will lead them to their hives. At night you can see festive fires along the horizon, and from the mountains you can hear the songs of the herdsmen who, I was told, got drunk for three straight days.

After the meal, cheered by the cithara and the singer Terpiade's joyful voice, Penelope and I looked each other in the eyes and discreetly, because of Telemachus, stood up to go to the rooms on the floor above. Naturally, the singer chose to mark this moment with certain wishes that made Penelope blush. So we quickened our pace and ran up the stairs in order to get out of earshot of the obscene allusions that singers always make toward newlyweds.

After all, wasn't this a second marriage? Neither I nor Penelope was the same as before. Adventures, shipwrecks, pain, solitude, deception, and in the end so much blood had shaped our souls and our faces, just as the wind and weather shape rocks. After so much confusion I kept repeating to myself that finally Penelope was Penelope and Odysseus was Odysseus. But simple things are not always true. I could sense how many doubts still unsettled Penelope's memories, even though she tried her best to hide them.

We pulled the curtain behind us at the top of the stairs, then locked the door to our bedroom, leaving the world outside.

The bed that I had described to Penelope in order to prove that I was Odysseus no longer looked the same way I had described it—it was practically unrecognizable, draped as it was with woolen cloth and lambskin. Time wears down men and things both, I said to myself, but I need to find a quick way to forget all of the suffering that afflicted my return to Ithaca and to escape from the unbearable series of illusions that I proved unable to master.

"We will stay locked in this room for one week without leaving it," I said to Penelope, who was laughing and crying simultaneously while I helped her undo her hair and take off her white linen dress. I could finally see her naked, the way I had remembered her in distant years in Ithaca, and later as she had appeared in my imagination. After so many fictions and disguises we were both naked on the bed and this was the only truth I clung to, like a shipwrecked sailor to a rock. I had almost shipwrecked here on my beloved Ithaca, and now I was finally safe, even if I was covered in wounds.

Penelope's face expressed all the happiness in the world, but streams of tears poured from her eyes, and she kept crying even when we intertwined on the bed in all the positions that our desires and our energy urged, and we covered ourselves in kisses and bites all night long. Finally freed from memories. We exhausted all of our desires on that old olive tree bed, which creaked beneath us like the planks of a ship on the waves of the sea. But from each desire another was born, and then yet another. I entered and came out of Penelope's body, and she was my tireless and willing partner in passion.

We left a candle burning in the room in order to look at each other, and to make the delights of love increase through our looks. Her loud moans of pleasure mixed with the cries of seagulls flying happily around the palace, as if they wanted to celebrate our new marriage and our amorous play.

"I'm glad the seagulls are covering my voice," Penelope said, "because my moans of love are for your ears only, just you, and nobody else."

PENELOPE

I suggested to Odysseus that he should not waste the memories of his adventures, from the war in Troy to his return to Ithaca and our reconciliation after the massacre of the Suitors. Odysseus welcomed my suggestion enthusiastically, and now while Telemachus takes an interest in restoring the city and working in the countryside, he spends his days in the company of the singer Terpiade, composing verses for two poems. The first about the Trojan War, so as to celebrate the memorable feats of the heroes, though in truth Odysseus detests them, and the second about his adventures on the return voyage to Ithaca up to our reunion, where he can finally give free rein to his imagination.

And then I thought, Why shouldn't I take a nice voyage too? When he finishes the first poem I will ask Odysseus to take me to Egypt. I've heard marvelous things about that country and I haven't left Ithaca once since I got married, as though it was my prison. Is it only men who have the right to travel?

"Composing these poems is exhausting," Odysseus said to me one day. "Achilles, Hector, Agamemnon, Ajax, and the other heroes are such insipid men, but my poem has to be as salty as seawater. I hope it works out the same way as with river water, which has no salt in it but makes the sea salty."

"It's the facts that count," I told Odysseus, "not their explanations. We don't know why the sea is salty, but it's enough to know that it is."

Obviously Odysseus didn't agree. He told me that every fact has its explanation, that he always tries to understand and, when he can't, invent a credible explanation. He says that credibility is one facet of the truth. I didn't want to start an argument, because I would have had to tell him that, when all was said and done, he didn't understand the first thing about Penelope.

The rains have finally arrived, cooling the air and soaking the arid, dusty ground. Everyone is happy, but the only thing Odysseus thinks about anymore is his Trojan story. Every now and then he leaves Terpiade alone and comes to speak with me about his poem.

"I have discovered that it is easier to fight a war than to tell stories about one. What am I saying, it is easier to tell stories about a war than to fight one."

Odysseus struggles with this contradiction between telling and doing, he is restless, but fortunately he never speaks about leaving, in spite of Tiresias' dire prediction. I hope that for him, telling his adventures is the same thing as living them. In the meantime, the two poems seem to take up all his energy and his indefatigable desire to tell stories, and to lie.

When the cobbler, tired of keeping the two boots in his warehouse and anxious to receive payment for his work, brought them to me, we decided to burn them. But after praising their solid craftsmanship, Odysseus put them on his feet, because before burning them, he said, he had a mission to accomplish.

Shivers ran through me and I was struck dumb.

"Don't worry," he said to me with a smile, "because I will be back before sundown with the precious gifts that I received from the king of the Phaeacians, which I hid on the beach where I landed. I couldn't bring them with me because everyone would have thought I was one of those pirates who infest the seas and the coasts, searching for booty. Now I will go and get those gold and silver objects and we will make a fine show of them in the great hall."

I relaxed at those words. I didn't want to fall prey to the suspicion of a new trick, not even for an instant. I have shown too much loving dedication during these delirious nights for the idea of leaving me, or Ithaca, to have even passed through his mind. Our bed has become a battleground, and I indulge Odysseus in all his desires because I am in love and his desires are mine as well. I think that his most uninhibited passions were taught to him by Calypso. All I can be is thankful to Calypso, because she has made our union more solid and certainly more lasting.

I am unconcerned, and if once again I have doubted Odysseus, I am ashamed of it.

ODYSSEUS

I crossed the newly sun-drenched island at a quick pace down a well-worn hunting path through thick woods, headed for the sea. At one point a large wild boar sow crossed my path with three piglets following her, but I did not regret having left my bow at home. I would never have shot a mother leading her babies around to teach them how to feed themselves. No sensible hunter would have.

Upon finally reaching a point where I could see the sea, I ran down to the beach and arrived at the cave where I had hidden my treasure at the foot of an old wild olive tree. I pulled back the branches and the stones that covered it and found the shiny golden cups and the other gifts from the king of the Phaeacians. I put the items into a hemp cloth in order to start the return trip. But there, lifting my eyes, I saw a ship passing along the coastline. A fast ship, one of those that merchants use for long voyages to barter or sell their goods. I saw the sailors on the deck looking at the coast, perhaps to find a landing spot for a rest.

The sea was slightly choppy and a light wind from Euros swelled the sails of the ship. I envied those sailors who traverse the seas in all seasons, and I said to myself that a spiteful god had sent that ship to tempt my destiny. Every time I see the sea my heart swells with desire, I close my eyes and can already see myself on the deck of a ship with the salty wind caressing my face; I can picture the long nights under a starry sky when the sea is calm and the warm air lulls you to sleep. Only those who have sailed much and have crossed the seas in calm and in tempest can know the joy that the sea instills in a sailor's soul.

Now all I would have to do is raise a shiny golden cup and show it to the sailors leaning over the deck, and the ship would stop here in the bay and I could join them and furrow the sea toward new, distant lands. The sky, the sea, the breeze and the wind that swell the sails, the sun, the pale moon in the warm, quiet nights, and then fishing for fish to roast on the embers.

Under the windy walls of Troy the heroes ate nothing but roasted meat, like the gods who appreciate sacrifices of meat but disapprove of fish. Those heroic warriors were constantly hungry, and had to plunder the defenseless herdsmen of the plains, while I and my companions ate our fill of fish. But I am a seafaring man.

Now the ship is approaching because I raised my arm to show a shiny golden cup, and the sailors are waving to me and I can hear their voices inviting me to come on board. Maybe my destiny is on the sea if the gods sent this ship and induced me to show the golden cup. Will I board that ship? What does my sailor's heart say? I close my eyes so as not to see the approaching ship.

No, my sailing friends, I will not come with you. I envy you, but I won't come with you. Penelope is waiting for me and Telemachus is too young to rule the island by himself. And Terpiade? Why on earth would I have spared his life if not to compose those two poems that I can already see clearly in my mind? The temptation of the sea is awesome, but I resisted the song of the Sirens before, and I won't let myself be seduced by a merchant ship now.

I put the golden cup back in the cloth, hefted the Phaeacian treasure to my shoulders, and quickly started off without looking back again, followed by my shadow along the hunting path.

The sun had already set when I arrived at the palace. I stopped in my tracks once again before entering, but Penelope came toward me and embraced me as if I had returned home from a long voyage. We stood there embracing for a long time and she held me tight as if she feared I could slip away from her.

"I was afraid you wouldn't come back."

"I didn't think about starting out on a voyage even for a second, let the gods be my witnesses. The sea has betrayed me too many times and is of no importance to me any longer. This is my truth."

I laid out the gifts from the Phaeacians on a table for Penelope to see. The bronze sword with the silver hilt, which Penelope looked at, pretending to admire it in order to please me, and then four splendid golden cups engraved with figures, three large silver platters, and a few jewelry boxes. In all, thirteen precious objects, as many as the kings of the Phaeacians.

"These objects will be included in our royal treasure, and we will make use of the golden cups and silver platters when we have worthy guests."

"No second thoughts?" Penelope asked.

"No second thoughts."

I finally took the boots off my feet and we burned them together with a handful of salt to ward off any future temptation to leave.

PENELOPE

Odysseus made me a solemn promise.

"My father Laertes is a gardener king. From now on, I will be a barefoot king."

"So you will stay in Ithaca."

"I will stay in Ithaca forever. The gods are my witnesses."

He made me another promise. That Helen will have a small part in the poem about the Trojan War, certainly smaller than the part that I will have in the poem about the return to Ithaca.

Sometimes I hear the sounds of long and heated disputes coming from below. It's a constant argument between Odysseus and Terpiade, and I am always worried that Odysseus will take up his sword and then, goodbye poem. Terpiade is a stubborn man and would like Odysseus to only tell the stories of things that really happened, but for Odysseus, every story that he tells has happened—he cannot distinguish between truth and fiction. And, after all, when has poetry ever spoken about truth? Poetry has inside itself a truth that is not of this world, but which comes from the mind of the poet and of the listener.

Odysseus does not want me to be near them while he works with Terpiade, if you can call composing verses work. For him, war and poetry are things fit for men alone. And so I sometimes hide behind the curtain at the top of the stairs and listen.

The beginning of the first poem, the one about the war in Troy, is resounding and dramatic, just as it should be in order to please the crowds in the markets and squares.

Wrath, goddess, sing of Achilles Peleus' son's
calamitous wrath, which hit the Achaeans with countless ills...

Achilles is the only hero from the Achaean camp whom Odysseus likes, perhaps because, like him, he tried everything he could to avoid participating in that wretched war, but then fought valorously. I want to see what will happen, on the other hand, with Agamemnon and Menelaus, whom Odysseus detests.

Notwithstanding the arguments with Terpiade, I am sure that Odysseus is quite determined to finish this poetic undertaking because his memory will be entrusted to it. And mine as well.

POSTSCRIPT

It is said that ancient Bronze Age myths are still told today by herdsmen in the mountains of Crete, of the Dodecanese, and of Cyprus. A few years ago in Corfu, which some have claimed is the island of the Phaeacians, a little old man seated on a stool on the corner of a street near the harbor told ancient stories and tales of love and death for a few drachmas. Among these, the colorful events of a warrior king who returns home victoriously after a long siege and a very long voyage across the Mediterranean, and who finds neighboring princes on his island who have taken up residence inside his palace and hope to marry his wife, the queen. The names of the characters were not, in the old man's tale, those of the Homeric heroes, but it was not hard to understand that he was talking about Odysseus, Penelope, and the Suitors, who were in fact killed off in his story, just as in the Homeric poem.

It came to mind, then, that it might still be possible to take these stories of Odysseus and Penelope directly from the popular tradition and tell them in new words, carrying them across nearly three millennia into the age of electronic communication and placing them alongside the written epic.

But there was another, more private and domestic moment that made me reconsider the story of Odysseus and his encounter with Penelope after his return to Ithaca. One evening at Cornell University in Ithaca, New York, I was talking about Homer and some of the narrative discrepancies in his works with Pietro Pucci, a professor of ancient Greek who had written books of important literary scholarship on the Homeric poems. At a certain point during the conversation, my wife, Anna, made an observation that stunned both myself and the scholar of Homer.

Penelope, my wife said, had immediately understood that Odysseus was hiding beneath the clothes of a beggar, but she wanted to pretend not to for a little while in order to make him pay for his amorous adventures during his return voyage, as well as for the lack of trust that had made him reveal himself to Telemachus and the old nurse Eurycleia but not to her. All in all, here was a tale of love and jealousy and conjugal intrigues that was waiting to be interpreted and rewritten for contemporary readers. This interpretation helps resolve another peculiarity: the dog Argos recognizes Odysseus, but Penelope does not.

The tale by the storyteller of Corfu, but more significantly this feminine insight, convinced me to rewrite the story of Odysseus and Penelope, and to take a few liberties in deviating from the Homeric tale in order to highlight not so much Odysseus' famous cunning as his emotional weaknesses, as well as Penelope's affectionate cunning and pride. Assuredly a less passive character than what a superficial reading of the *Odyssey* might lead us to believe, a reading that has created an inaccurate and slightly boring idea of this sublime fictional character.

At the end of my tale I wanted to go out on a limb with my own personal conjecture about the origin of the *Iliad* and the *Odyssey,* or at the very least about the primitive versions of the two poems. Who better than an ingenious protagonist like Odysseus could tell those stories about war, about adventure, and about love? Isn't there perhaps proof of this in the stories he told in the palace of Alcinous?

This is a poetic theory, but not really so absurd when you consider that in an anonymous text that scholars have dated to the fourth century B.C.E. and that is known as the *Contest of Homer and Hesiod* (it talks, in fact, about a poetic competition between Hesiod and Homer), it is said that the author of the *Iliad* and the *Odyssey* was actually the son of Telemachus, and that he had simply written down a family legend. What's more, the ancient anonymous text mentions a woman in Ithaca who had been sold as a slave by the Phoenicians, and speaks of her as if she were Homer's mother. We are circling around Ithaca and the family of Odysseus like a diviner slowly closing in on underground water.

Odysseus as the author of the two epics, is this not the simplest and most seductive hypothesis?

L. M.

Founded in 1893,
UNIVERSITY OF CALIFORNIA PRESS
publishes bold, progressive books and journals
on topics in the arts, humanities, social sciences,
and natural sciences—with a focus on social
justice issues—that inspire thought and action
among readers worldwide.

The UC PRESS FOUNDATION
raises funds to uphold the press's vital role
as an independent, nonprofit publisher, and
receives philanthropic support from a wide
range of individuals and institutions—and from
committed readers like you. To learn more, visit
ucpress.edu/supportus.